SMOKE AND MIRRORS

THE DIVISION BOOK 1

ANGUS MCLEAN

Published 2015 by Smoking Gun Publications

ISBN 978-0473560843

Copyright © Angus McLean 2015

The right of Angus McLean to be identified as the author of this work has been asserted by the author in accordance with the Copyright Act 1994.

The story contained within this book is a work of fiction. Names and characters are the product of the author's imagination and any resemblance to actual persons, living or dead, is entirely coincidental.

All rights reserved. No part of this book may be reproduced, stored in or introduced into a retrieval system, or transmitted in any form, or by any means (electronic, electrostatic, magnetic tape, mechanical, photocopying, recording or otherwise) without the prior written permission of the publisher. Any person who does any unauthorised act in relation to this publication may be liable to criminal prosecution and civil claims for damages.

ALSO BY ANGUS MCLEAN

Early Warning Series

Martial Law

Getting Home

Stand Fast

The Division Series

Smoke and Mirrors

Call to Arms

The Shadow Dancers

The Berlin Conspiracy

No Second Chance

Chase Investigations Series

Old Friends

Honey Trap

Sleeping Dogs

Tangled Webs

Dirty Deeds

Red Mist

Fallen Angel

Holy Orders

Deal Breaker

Nicki Cooper Mystery Series

The Country Club Caper

SMOKE AND MIRRORS
BY ANGUS MCLEAN

1

Baghdad, Iraq
Two years ago

It wasn't called the Highway to Hell for nothing.
Driving on the highway from the city to Baghdad International Airport was like 200 miles of dodgems, only every dodgem potentially carried a bomb or a carload of ruthless bastards who wanted to slice off your head on Al-Jazheera and drag your corpse through the streets.

Archer loved it and loathed it at the same time; the thrill of the risk was intoxicating, but the reality of it going bad was too terrifying to contemplate. In his team of PMCs they had a deal – last man standing finished any wounded then took one himself.

Deny the pricks the pleasure of doing it themselves.

His team, he thought to himself. For about another hour, they were still his team. After that he was on a big bird to LA to meet up with a tidy American Army Major, to spend 3 weeks eating, drinking and screwing, in no particular order. After 3 weeks R&R he was coming back, and they'd be his team again.

He cast a lazy eye to the driver on his right, big Grunter, a bald former SWAT team officer in Johannesburg. He was built like a house and ate constantly when he wasn't working out. He had seen more action in Jo'burg than most squaddies in Iraq. He drove the Nissan Patrol like it was a Tonka toy.

Behind Grunter sat Jacko, a former Para sergeant who had served a full 20 years and gone straight into the private sector to earn his pension. The Brit was a tattooed chain smoker and notorious practical-joker. Archer's boxers still scratched from when Jacko had drowned them in starch and turned them to cardboard.

In the rear of the wagon was the gunner, on this occasion Bula, the Fijian alcoholic who had served with 22 SAS for a decade before going private. Constantly smiling and hung over he was nearly fifty and the veteran of a dozen wars around the globe.

Archer kept his eyes moving, scanning his arc to the left, the barrel of his Russian AK-47 resting on his left knee, finger alongside the trigger guard, stock folded for ease of movement. Vehicles all around them, moving like people on a conveyer belt, an endless stream towards the airport and its surrounds. Iraqis stared back at the white faces with either indifference or open disdain and hostility. Not fear. These people were not afraid of the heavily armed men in the packet, identical in their polo shirts and wrap around shades. Men like this had come and gone, and would always do so, and it meant nothing. They meant nothing; just another white face.

The sun was at a dangerous angle, and Grunter was squinting behind his shades and the sun visor. The white Renault in front of them carried their other team members and their clients, a pair of oil company execs who had spent a week schmoozing and were on their way home. Archer was accompanying them, which suited the team because they could tie in the drop-off with picking up a new team member on his way in from the UK. Dusty, up front with his fellow former Royal Marine, Tim, would be running the team in Archer's absence. He was a good man but probably a little more conservative than Archer would have liked. Although conservative wasn't always a bad thing in this part of the world.

Dusty was giving the constant commentary that they could hear over their earpieces, identifying any risks or potential trouble spots as they came into range.

'White truck, right, 150. Man in back with AK. 100 now, not aware. Closing up, still not aware...'

Bula's voice came over the radio then.

'Hey, red Beamer coming from behind, left of us, 3 or 4 boys. Unfriendlies, keeping eyes.'

Archer caught sight in the wing mirror of the BMW coming up on the left, two boys in the front and at least another in the back. All of them had eyes on the Patrol, and he could see the tension in their bodies.

At the same time, Dusty came back on.

'Dead dog, right, 100.'

IED, thought Archer, thumbing off his safety catch at the same time.

'Drop back Grunter,' he ordered and felt the Patrol slow immediately, 'eyes up guys. I've got the left, keep your arcs.'

The red BMW was almost even with them now and he could see two in the back now. The angle was no good for seeing weapons though. He rested his finger lightly on the trigger and kept one eye on the car and one on the rest of the surrounds. The gap between the Patrol and the Renault had opened up slightly, allowing them more room to move in an IA.

Archer saw a flicker of movement from the back seat as the closest passenger lifted the barrel of an AK into view. All eyes from the car were on his now in his wing mirror and he knew it was game on.

'Grunter, hit it!' he barked, the AK coming into view properly as the window came down. He raised his own AK as Grunter jerked the wheel left and smashed into the front wing of the Beamer.

Archer triggered a burst through the window straight into the interior of the car as it lurched to the left, at the same time as an almighty explosion erupted from the right, strong enough to rock the Patrol and blow out windows in the cars around it. The windscreen shattered under the force of debris and Archer felt stings across his face and arm.

Traffic closed up all around them as cars crashed into each other, and Grunter jerked the wheel left again, smashing into a beaten up pick up that had drifted in front of him. He gunned the big engine and shoved the pick up out of the way, clearing a space to get to the shoulder of the road. The white Renault was also moving left, seeking a way clear of the carnage.

Archer saw the BMW coming back, accelerating up on the left, openly displaying AKs out the windows now.

'Contact left! Contact left!' he barked into his mouthpiece, one hand depressing the pressel switch on his chest and the other levelling the AK. He cut loose another burst, longer this time, raking the windscreen of the BMW to blind the driver. Jacko had slid across the backseat and opened up too, a long burst into the back which took out the closest passenger.

Too late, he realised they had made the wrong move, both vehicles coming to the left.

A second explosion detonated on the shoulder of the road, bigger than the first and almost directly in front of the Renault. The front of the car lifted off the ground in a shower of dust and dirt and flame, crashing back down at an angle and almost rolling, rocking on its springs as it settled back down again at the edge of a smoking crater.

Grunter was blinded and ran straight into the back of the Renault, shunting it forward before he managed to stop.

Surrounded by a dust cloud and with screams in his ears, Archer shouted, 'Debus, debus! IA!'

He threw the door open and leaped out, snapping open the butt stock of the AK and shouldering it, seeking targets.

The boys in the BMW knew they were there and would be using the Patrol as a start point, so they needed to get clear quickly, secure the guys from the Renault, and move.

Archer moved forward as per their IA drills, bellowing, 'Moving!' and making a magazine change on the run.

He got to the wreck of the Renault and wrenched open the left rear door. He could see immediately that the two execs were shaken and scratched but okay. Dusty was bleeding in the front passenger's seat, the front of his armour saturated from a wound in his face. Tim was dead, most of his head gone and sprayed across the execs in the back.

Archer seized the closest client by the arm and yanked him out, shouting, 'Move! Move now!'

Gunfire sounded behind him above the heavy buzz in his ears but he ignored it, focussing on the task at hand. The exec tumbled out and Archer pushed him to the ground a couple of metres away with an order to stay down. The second one was frozen and wouldn't budge. Archer grabbed him by the collar and jerked him across the back seat but he locked his arms and legs against the door frame and began wailing like a scared child.

Not breaking stride, Archer thumped him in the face with a left jab and stunned him, then yanked him out and pushed him down beside his mate. Kneeling over them he scanned around, seeing the BMW pulled up near the Patrol, all doors open and fire coming from behind it. Jacko and Grunter were deployed at each end of the Patrol, trading shots with the Beamer boys. Bula was cutting around another vehicle, the RPK in his hands looking like a .22 to a normal sized man. He was seeking an angle to out flank the enemy.

Archer slapped both execs on the head and shouted at them to stay down, then pushed up and returned to the Renault. The front passenger door was buckled and wouldn't open. He used his rifle barrel to clear the broken glass and reached in to Dusty. The former Marine was barely conscious, bleeding heavily from a nasty gouge to his left cheek and another slice across his forehead. His nose looked broken, and Archer realised he had probably smashed his face into the dash. A quick check revealed no other obvious injuries.

'Come on you whinging fuckin' Pom!'

Archer slung his AK and grabbed his mate under the arms, heaving him up and dragging him through the window. He dragged him across to the execs and lay him down. Ripping Dusty's own field dressing from his webbing Archer pressed it against the cheek wound and used his arm to wipe some of the blood away. He ripped a length of duct tape from his own webbing and secured it across the dressing and half way round Dusty's head.

He checked the lads again and saw Bula had got distracted. Somebody had opened up from the far side of the road at him, and he had now taken a knee behind a vehicle and was trying to pick off the target through the wreckage around him.

Archer moved right, keeping well clear of his own lads' arcs, AK in the shoulder. He could see two of the Beamer boys behind the engine block, each with an AK, taking turns to rise and pop a short burst at Jacko and Grunter.

Archer dropped flat on his belly and took aim. He could see the side of one of the boys around the edge of the wrecked BMW, and let loose a quick double tap. A scream sounded and the gunman fell backwards into full view. Archer gave him a longer burst that shook him like a bad disco dancer and he dropped his AK, writhing in the dirt. His mate wasn't stupid though and kept his position behind the engine block, his feet hidden by the wheel.

Archer saw his gun barrel poke up above the bonnet of the BMW and readied himself. The gun edged up horizontally and loosed off a spray of rounds blindly, the bullets sweeping across the side of the Patrol and punching more holes in it.

Jacko was closest to Archer and returned a burst of his own, before yelling, 'Stoppage!'

Archer saw him ripping his magazine off and slapping in a new one, then yanking at the bolt.

'Stoppage!' he shouted again, indicating a jam.

The other Beamer boy obviously understood some English because he saw his opportunity to seal the deal. Archer rose at the same time as the insurgent and double tapped him in the chest. The Iraqi fell back behind the car, his AK firing wildly into the sky.

'Moving!'

Archer moved forward and right, seeing the three Iraqis behind the car. One dead on his back, the second rolling on his side with the

AK still in his hand, trying to bring it round, the third at the back trading shots with Grunter.

He put a burst into the wounded gunman, the third oblivious to his presence, and moved in closer. The third gunman saw him now and swung round to meet the new threat, but too late. As he moved, Grunter took his head off at the shoulders with a triple burst, and Archer caught him in the front as he went down.

Archer put another burst into the head of the first man, and repeated it on the second. Grunter had moved forward now and finished off what was left of his own target.

More gunfire sounded from the roadway, a couple of single AK shots then a sustained burst of machine gun fire.

Bula came back through the dust at a jog, the RPK in his hands and blood dribbling from his leg. He was still grinning.

'Got 'im bro,' he shouted, taking a knee near Jacko, covering arcs again.

'Grunter, get the wagon going,' Archer ordered, 'Jacko with me. Bula; with Grunter.'

They moved quickly, Jacko covering the growing crowd of onlookers as Archer got to the execs and Dusty.

He took a knee over them and covered an arc, hearing horn blasts and roaring Humvee engines as an American PMC team approached from the rear. There were smashing sounds as the column forced its way through the traffic, even though it would have been easier to go wide into the desert.

Not much difference between some of the PMCs and their service comrades, Archer thought.

Grunter got the Patrol going and manoeuvred fully onto the shoulder, Bula trotting behind him as he made his way forward. They quickly loaded the execs into the backseat and onto the floor, Jacko over them.

Archer got Dusty into the back as well then moved back to the Renault. Bula got a Union Jack out and slung it across the back of the Patrol to face the Yanks when they arrived. The last thing they wanted now was friendly fire.

Tim's legs were stuck under the steering wheel and Archer was working at freeing them, trying to ignore the sticky mess around him, when he heard the Yank packet arrive. He got the right leg free and got Tim half out the window when he heard a burst of fire.

Cradling Tim in his arms he threw a glance over his shoulder, instinct telling him this was going bad.

A Humvee was pulled up near the Patrol, and a gunner was leaning out the window with his M4, shouting at Bula who stood near the back of the Patrol with his RPK.

'Oh shit...'

Archer let Tim down and started to move back to his team, waving and shouting at the soldier, but it was too late.

The gunner was obviously amped up and used to giving orders that were obeyed. Bula was also amped up but still in control, but that wasn't the problem. He was holding a machine gun and had dark skin, and even though Archer clearly understood he was shouting 'Security patrol! We're on your side!' the young Yank obviously couldn't understand a Fijian accent.

The M4 burst off rounds and Bula went down.

'Fuck!'

Archer sprinted forward now, hands in the air, shouting, 'Cease fire! Cease fire!'

He got to the roadway and the Humvee emptied out. The gunslinger who had shot Bula darted towards him with his carbine raised, ready to finish him, convinced he had taken a Taleban down.

'Stand down you fuckin' moron!' Jacko bellowed at him, debussing with Grunter, both of them wise enough to leave their AKs behind.

The gunner swung his rifle towards them then paused as the two white men confronted him. His gaze went back to where Bula lay still in the dust.

'What the hell...'

He never finished his sentence because Grunter seized him by the throat with one big mitt and stripped him of his weapon with the other. He lifted the other guy onto his tip-toes and tossed the carbine aside.

Jacko went to Bula and Archer reached them just as the vehicle commander, a young surfer looking dude, pointed a rifle at Grunter's head.

'Stand down, boy,' he drawled, calm and quiet. 'Do it now.'

Grunter tossed the gunner aside like a rag doll and stepped back, hands raised and his face as impassive as ever. Jacko stood and came over. He had blood on his hands and rage in his eyes.

'He's dead,' he said flatly. He raised his hands to shoulder height, showing the blood on his hands to the Americans.

Archer sucked in a breath through his nose and felt grit in his eyes. The American squad were facing them, guns raised. Compared to his own team, these guys were the stereotypical private contractors in a company uniform of desert boots, sand khakis and navy blue polos, all with fingerless gloves, baseball caps and wrap around shades. Their armour vests were loaded with radios, spare mags and bulging pouches.

Archer recognised them straight away as Black Star operators. Known on the circuit as Death Star due to the high number of lives they both lost and took, they had a terrible reputation for questionable contacts. A couple of their guys were awaiting trial for wiping out an unarmed family in Fallujah the previous year. They were the last guys he wanted to tangle with when everyone was already hot under the collar.

He knew for a fact that many of their guys were either shell shocked vets who should never have been trusted with a gun again, or former soldiers who had been dishonourably discharged. Drug use was apparently rife among their ranks and allegations of looting had been made.

'We're private security,' he told the team leader, 'we've got clients on board and got hit by a couple of IEDs. We've got one KIA and a casualty on board; we could do with a medic.'

His gaze shifted to the gunner who'd shot Bula, standing aside rubbing his throat and eyeing Grunter resentfully.

'Now we've got two KIAs, thanks to you.'

'Ahh thought he's a Taleban,' the guy whined to his commander. 'All them rag heads look the same, sarge.'

'He's Fijian, you fuckin' Dixie inbreed,' Jacko growled, his nostrils flaring.

The gunner also flared, and stepped forward.

'Who you callin' inbreed, boy?'

'Sergeant, call him off,' Archer warned, deliberately using the team leader's previous rank. He put a hand on Jacko's arm. 'Leave it Jacko.'

'Private!'

'I ain't no Dixie...'

They were nearly toe to toe now.

'Sergeant, control your man,' Archer said forcefully, taking a step forward.

Jacko's fist flashed out and flattened the young gunner's nose across his face, and Archer moved between them, pushing them both back. He turned, holding Jacko back, just in time to catch a jab from the gunner in the side of his face.

He shook it off, opened his mouth to speak again, and took another jab.

Enough's enough.

His own right uppercut came up full force and collected the Black Star gunman under his jaw, lifting him onto his toes and knocking him backwards with his eyes rolling back in his head.

A rifle butt smashed into the side of Archer's skull and everything went black.

2

The Landon Hotel in downtown Auckland had played host to many notable politicians, celebrities and members of royalty over the years.

For the last month it had also played host to Yassar Al-Riyaz, accompanied by a team of minders and an ongoing procession of highly paid whores. Yassar occupied the penthouse suite, ate his meals either in his room or in nearby top flight restaurants, and spent big at the casino. He bought the piles of meth that his whores smoked and ordered cases of champagne like it was soft drink.

Yassar was a peripheral member of the Saudi royal family, which didn't allow him a title but gave him plenty of insight into the machinations of terrorism and worldwide criminal enterprises. Even in a notoriously corrupt family, Yassar's branch was acknowledged as something else. Unlike more high-profile members of the family they made no attempt to hide their criminality, earning millions of tax-free dollars providing services to whoever could pay the bill; terrorists, drug dealers, people smugglers, it didn't matter. Cash was king and no questions were asked.

The minders were part of his father's crew, and as such Yassar trusted them like he would trust a cornered viper. He knew they fed intel back to his father on his every move, keeping the patriarch up to date with every latest development and scandal in his youngest son's embarrassing journey.

It annoyed him that he had no option but to keep them on; with no income of his own, Yassar relied on his father to fund his debauchery, while his older brothers actively contributed to the family business.

Until, that was, Yassar finally found his own niche a few short months ago. His financial sense was a family trait, but it was only from necessity that Yassar extended himself. A former IRA moneyman had approached him via another contact and struck a deal to supply arms to African guerrilla groups.

Yassar had begun siphoning off weapons from the shipments his elder brother Kali was shipping to Eastern Europe. A few crates of AK-47s here, a few crates of RPGs there. The money came in and the weapons went out. Before too long Yassar was getting bolder and approaching suppliers himself, undercutting his brother and even supplying weapons to the opponents of Kali's customers.

Everything was fair in business, he reasoned, until Kali stuck a .45 in his mouth and warned him in no uncertain terms to cease and desist immediately. Their father's answer was to send Yassar to New Zealand in disgrace to stay out of the way while Kali negotiated a particularly sensitive deal.

Sitting on the massive bed in his suite, Yassar stared at the laptop screen on his knees. The instant message in front of him was from his business partner, Patrick Boyle. They used private chat rooms to communicate, knowing that emails and phones were easily monitored. In coded speak the message outlined that the deal was ready to go as soon as Yassar replied. A shipment of heavy machine guns, mortars, rockets, ammunition and various other pieces of ordnance were currently in the bowels of a Burmese container ship bound for the Sudan.

Boyle had the ship's captain in his pocket and could divert the shipment to Somalia at a phone call. A Somalian warlord was eager to take the shipment himself and had an electronic transfer waiting for the push of a button.

The diversion would immediately scuttle Kali's deal, which would cause untold grief within the family, and probably a forthwith recall to face the music. Yassar sighed heavily, uncertain. A trickle of sweat ran down his bare chest. Despite Boyle's assurances that nobody would know of his involvement, he was certain that he would immediately be the prime suspect.

He knew of the arrangements and had passed the details to Boyle, who took care of the business end of things. He did not relish facing his father over this or, for that matter, Kali himself.

On the flipside however, pushing the button right now would net Yassar ten million pounds sterling of his own. *Ten million pounds*. Chickenfeed in Saudi terms but with that he could hide for a time while he went into business proper with Boyle. The man was smart and had plenty of contacts; together they could make a real fortune.

Yassar slowly typed a reply in the dialogue box.

Looking forward to catching up soon.

His trembling finger hovered over the Enter button. His heart beat wildly and he closed his eyes for a moment, procrastinating over probably the biggest decision of his life.

Fuck it, he decided. *Kali can go to hell. He's not the only smart one in our family.*

He hit Enter and sat back from the laptop, taking a deep breath.

A few seconds later a new dialogue box opened up from Boyle's end. No words, just a smiley face.

Yassar smiled despite his nerves and pushed the computer away. He felt better now. Bolder. More in control.

He clapped his hands happily and climbed off the bed. He was completely naked and needed a shower. But before that, he needed a release.

'Where are you, my lovely?' he called.

A few moments later the bedroom door opened and an equally naked blonde woman entered. She had implants and a Brazilian, a snake tattoo around her left ankle and a pierced navel. Her name was

Brittany and she'd spent the last three days in the suite, satisfying Yassar's every whim in the filthiest possible ways.

He ran his eye appreciatively over her body and felt a stirring within. She came to him and ran a long fingernail through his wispy chest hair.

'What would you like, sweetie pie?' she cooed. Her finger continued down and lightly brushed his member, causing him to twitch. 'Hmmm...I think I have an idea...'

As she dropped to her knees in front of him, Yassar ran a hand through her long hair and wondered how many of these he could buy with ten million pounds.

3

Archer woke in a sweat, his heart racing and his mind swimming with thoughts he couldn't grasp hold of, images that darted out of sight before he could see them. But he knew what they were.

He stared at the ceiling above him in the darkness, the fan circling lazily to keep the temperature down in the mid summer heat. The sheets around him were wet and smelled dank. His hair was wet and his bare skin was slick with it. The figure in the bed beside him was sleeping soundly, oblivious to his unrest.

Archer rolled silently from the bed and padded across the floor out to the kitchen. The moonlight bathed the back yard of the beach house and he stared out the window over the sink as he drained a glass of water. He refilled it and drank again, his pulse gradually slowing and his breathing returning to normal.

He took another draught of water and spilled some on his chin, letting the coolness dribble down into the hair on his chest. A light came on behind him and he saw her reflection in the kitchen window, leaning on the doorjamb, watching him. Long thick brown hair curled down to slim shoulders. The checked flannelette shirt was filled out nicely at the front and barely covered the womanly curve of her hips.

Archer heard her sigh and watched her cock her head to one side as she always did. He topped up the glass of water before turning to face her, unashamedly naked, neither of them at all self-conscious. He studied her silhouette, taking his time to work his way down her body and back up again, feeling her watching him throughout.

'Trouble sleeping?' she asked when his eyes again met hers.

Archer nodded silently, pushed himself away from the bench and moved to her, standing close enough to inhale her scent without touching her. Her hand came up to his chest and she ran her fingers through the hair there, reaching up and cupping his neck, drawing him down closer. Their lips met briefly before she pulled back again.

'Come to bed,' she told him, turning and leading the way back into the bedroom. Archer heard the bed creak as she lay down again, and he wondered fleetingly at the sense of what he was doing. She was a neighbour and friend, an occasional lover. Nothing more. But it was enough for him right now.

He followed her back to bed.

4

The Monaro was the 2005 model, a fire engine red VZ CV8 with a 346 cubic inch 5.7 litre V8. It drank petrol and rumbled like Muhammad Ali, but it was sleek and powerful and Archer loved driving it. It ate up the roads from his home in the small east coast town of Beachlands, hugging the corners and powering the straights, growling with pleasure as he worked his way through all six speeds, gunning it and tweaking it in equal measure, taking absolute pleasure in the masculine joy of driving a fast car fast.

He took a back road south and got to Walters Road on the rural edge of Takanini, before pulling in the driveway of the Papakura Army Base. The security guard on the gate recognised the car and started lifting the barrier arm before Archer had even come to a stop, but made a point of looking at the ID card he was shown anyway.

Archer eased past the gate and into the camp proper, keeping his speed low as he made his way past the various administration buildings into the heart of the camp. It was quiet this morning, just the odd vehicle and jogger about. One squadron was overseas, and the other would be split between various training exercises and smaller team jobs. The Commandos would be in place as normal, training for counter-terrorism scenarios.

He reached Rennie Lines, the home of 1NZSAS Group, and parked the Monaro in the staff car parking area. Crossing to the solid steel entrance gates, Archer swiped his access card and punched a PIN into the keypad before the pedestrian gate buzzed open, banging closed behind him again.

He made his way into the HQ building, nodding to a couple of regulars as they walked past on the way to the gym. They nodded back, not recognising him but knowing he must be one of the brotherhood to be where he was. It was not uncommon for regulars like them to not know reservists like him. Like Archer, the rest of the small reserve unit were former 'blades' who had left the regular force but maintained their skills through training, exercises and where possible full operational deployments.

Passing through reception, Archer ignored the side corridor that led to the individual squadron Interest Rooms and bounded up the stairs instead. The Group Adjutant's office was on the second floor along the corridor from the CO's office, and was much smaller.

Archer entered without knocking first, pausing to do so only once he was inside. The Adjutant looked up, a young Major with already-receding hair and a youthful face.

'Archie, good to see you,' he enthused, standing to shake Archer's hand.

Archer dropped into the chair across the desk and crossed his ankle over his knee.

'How're things, Troppo?'

The Major grinned and ran a hand through his hair. He was dressed in casual DPMs and had his hair longer than regulation length, as was normal with many operators. Troppo had gained his nickname years ago for catching not one but two tropical diseases while on an exercise in Asia, one having suspiciously similar symptoms to Chlamydia. It had taken quite some explaining to his new bride and was the subject of endless ribbing.

'Good mate, good. Just gearing up some of the boys for a joint exercise with the cops. All the usual admin shite, you know how it is.'

Archer did know, and it made him pleased he had never been an Adjutant. He'd done six years in the Group, starting with the standard couple of years as a Troop Commander after which he was expected to move into an admin role.

Operations had been his thing though, and with the commitments in Afghanistan he'd managed to stay in the thick of it for much longer than most officers. He had persuaded the CO to leave him running Mountain Troop then, when a vacancy rose on Air Troop, Archer had slid sideways into that.

It had caused ripples among some of the officers but Archer didn't care; he wanted trigger time. Tours to Afghanistan and Asia had been complemented by a controversial attachment to 22 for a year, allowing him to also go to Iraq, among other theatres. Much longer than the normal "long look" attachment, it had been experimental and highly sought after by more senior officers.

Archer had ended his tour as the most experienced, and the most decorated, Troop Commander in the unit. Refusing further promotion back to the regular force, where he would have to take his chances later against more administratively-minded sorts if he wanted to fight for one of the two Sabre Squadron Commander positions when they came up, he had instead gone private. The lure of high pay and higher risk had been too much to resist, and he had loved it until the day Bula died.

He shook the thought from his head angrily and focussed on the officer across the desk from him, who was still talking.

'So the Old Man wanted to see you about something,' he was saying, referring to the CO, 'he's got someone in with him but wanted you to go in as soon as you arrived.'

'Is that why I get a text from you at 7 in the morning?' Archer asked with some puzzlement, and Troppo grinned.

'Why, did you have company?'

Archer cracked a smile himself, reflecting briefly on the night that had passed.

'How is that neighbour of yours, anyway?'

Archer ignored the question and headed for the door.

'I better go and see the Old Man; no doubt he knows I'm here already.'

He made his way to the end of the hall, passing the mounted portraits of previous commanders reaching back to Major Frank Rennie in 1955. The current CO was the latest addition to the rogue's gallery, as it was known among the ruperts, and had been commander of the Group since partway through Archer's tenure.

Archer rapped on the solid oak door and paused, receiving a sharp 'Enter' from within. Stepping into the large office, Archer saw the CO standing by the window in full DPMs including the Group's bright blue stable belt. He was a tall, broad man with a slight stoop due to arthritis in his neck, prematurely grey and with a slight paunch. Word had it he was near the end of his term and in waiting for the top job in the Army.

He turned his head as Archer entered and nodded.

'Morning Craig,' he said, running a quick eye over the newcomer, noting the casual cargo pants and polo shirt. They seemed out of place in the office of perhaps the most powerful man in the military, but were commonplace in such a unit.

'Morning boss.' Archer nodded back, glancing to his right at the man standing by a book case. His face split into a grin and he stuck out his hand. 'Jedi! How are you?'

The other man grabbed his hand and pumped it once, bone crushingly hard, a smile crossing his face too. He was a small sandy haired man with not an ounce of fat on him, despite being now in his late forties. Known as Jedi, Jed Ingoe was a former Regimental Sergeant Major, with a fearsome reputation. He had served with distinction all over the globe and was renowned as one of the hardest men to ever wear the sand coloured beret.

His active soldiering had ended during Archer's last tour of Afghanistan when he lost his left leg to an IED.

'Good to see you Craig. How've you been?'

'Very good thank you. This is not a social visit then?' he enquired of the CO.

'No, not at all. Take a seat.'

The CO went behind his desk and Archer joined Ingoe across from him in the visitors' chairs. Archer noted that Jedi seemed more comfortable now with his prosthetic limb than when he'd last seen him a year ago.

'Everything went okay in Indonesia?' the CO enquired, and Archer nodded, not realising the boss had even known he'd been there. It had been a short job, just a month doing risk assessments and CP work for an aid agency, and he'd been back only a couple of days.

'No problem, boss. Things are the same as ever over there.'

The CO nodded again, not an emotion to be seen in his face. He liked to keep an eye on his troops, and also liked them to know it.

'We have the annual Lawman exercise coming up, as you know,' he said, 'and you were earmarked for a role in it, like last year.'

Archer said nothing, noting the use of the past tense 'were.' Lawman was an annual joint Army-Police CT exercise, and last year he had been stuck in a backroom role which he had hated.

'However.' The CO cleared his throat and turned towards Ingoe. 'The RSM has something to discuss with you.'

Archer shifted in his seat for a better angle towards Ingoe.

'Do you know what I've been doing since I left the Group?' Ingoe asked.

Archer twitched his head. 'I've heard a whisper.'

'Of?'

'That you were working for a government department on security issues.'

Ingoe inclined his own head.

'Something like that,' he said. 'Obviously everything that gets said in this room stays here. The boss has clearance, but nobody else here knows, or needs to know, anything. Right?'

'Of course.'

Ingoe paused before continuing, obviously selecting his words carefully.

'I have been tasked to speak to you. I have a shortlist of people to speak to, and you are just one of them. The people on that list have all been selected by myself and one or two others with the relevant knowledge.'

Archer waited, feeling a thrill run through his core.

'I need to ask you two things.' Ingoe held his gaze calmly. 'Firstly, are you interested in a government role?'

'It would depend on what it was,' Archer replied carefully, 'if it's what I think it probably is, then yes.'

'Okay.' Ingoe considered that for a moment. 'Secondly, if you were to take it, are you available immediately?'

Archer rubbed his jaw.

'I'm available now, but I do have work lined up in a couple of weeks. I may be going back to Jakarta.'

Ingoe nodded again, looking away for a minute. Archer saw him make eye contact with the CO, who gave the tiniest incline of his head. Ingoe turned back to Archer.

'It's a field role suited to your skill set, based in Auckland but with an international flavour. It's attached to the department I work for, but appears on no org chart anywhere. For all intents and purposes, it does not exist. Understand?'

'Absolutely.'

The thrill got faster in Archer's gut, and he squeezed his fists together.

'If you were to take the role, you would be classed as a case officer, with Top Secret clearance. There would be various training requirements to meet, however the role would commence almost immediately with a task that needs urgent attention. Clear?'

'Crystal.'

Ingoe nodded slowly.

'Interested?'

Archer felt a smile break his lips.

'Of course.'

5

The suite reeked of sweat, sex and methamphetamine smoke.
Cody could feel the light burning through her eyelids and screwed her eyes shut harder, fighting consciousness for as long as she could.

After a week in this room she was wrecked. She'd smoked more drugs and had more sex than she'd had in the previous month. The Arab dude, Chester or whatever the fuck he called himself, was a fucking demon. He was high most of the time and fucked anything with a heartbeat.

Last night she'd done a 69er with Chanelle while he watched, and she wasn't even a lesbo; Chanelle didn't care, she was off her tits anyway.

Fuck that chick could smoke a lot.

After the 69er Chester had fucked each of them then let a couple of his bodyguards have a crack as well.

Cody was sweet with that – one of the guards was kinda cute anyway, in a camel-jockey sorta way – so she'd blown him and let Chanelle have the ugly one.

Today was her last day though, and she was looking forward to getting home. Home to her shitty apartment in Mt Eden and her shitty boyfriend pissing and moaning and wanting to know how much dick she'd had that wasn't his own.

You'd be counting that in metres, honey.

Fuckin' Bad-Bad Leroy Brown – that was actually his name, thanks to wastoid parents – and his pansy-assed whingey little boy routine.

Cody rolled on her side and opened her eyes properly. Chanelle was passed out on the other side of the king-sized bed, naked as a jaybird and with her bleached hair all over the place. A tattoo of a snake slithered up her left leg from the ankle, wrapping itself around like a branch, and ended with a flickering tongue reaching for her pussy.

Chester thought it was cool; Cody thought it was fuckin' stupid. Most of the girls from the agency had tattoos of some sort – it's not the sort of industry that attracts prissy librarians, right? – and Cody was particularly proud of the pair of tumbling dice on her hip. It was a reminder of the first time a client had attacked her, when she was just a naive sixteen year old runaway selling her gash on K Rd. Every interaction was a roll of the dice. Sometimes luck went your way; sometimes it didn't.

As Cody's focus came back and the meth haze started to clear from her head, she became aware of somebody else in the room. Her gaze shifted slightly and she saw Chester standing at the end of the bed, holding a cell phone up and smirking to himself as he filmed Chanelle's unconscious form. He was naked too, and obviously aroused by whatever the fuck he was doing.

What the fuck is he doing?

She shifted her gaze again to Chanelle and took a moment to realise. The other girl was on her back, legs spread and arms splayed to the sides. Perching on her crotch was a full grown mouse, white and whiskery, slowly nibbling a chunk of cheese. It was facing towards the tattooed snake. From where Chester stood it would look like the snake was about to eat the mouse.

Cody grimaced to herself and watched the mouse with

fascination. It looked lethargic, like it was drugged or something. Probably was. Chester had a fuckin' medicine cabinet with him. More than once in the last week she'd woken up with someone fucking her, and she knew she hadn't been that out of it. The other girls had said the same.

He was one weird fuckin' dude.

He must've sensed her looking because his head snapped around and his eyes darkened as he looked at her.

'I wondered who would wake up first,' he said, switching the phone off and tossing it onto a chair. He came towards her. 'Just having a little fun, baby.' He started to climb onto the bed at her feet. 'Party time for you and me, baby. She can sleep a bit longer.'

Cody pushed herself up into a sitting position and slid backwards a bit, giving him pause. 'Party time's over, baby. Today's a new day.' She rubbed her fingers together to indicate cash. 'Time is money, honey. If you got the money...'

'I pay you for today,' he retorted. 'Already done.'

'No baby, you paid me up until this morning.' She sensed him getting angry and tried a softer approach. 'But we can deal again, it's all good.' She smiled now. 'I'll just go have a shower while you get some cash and then we'll party, okay?'

'No!' Chester's tone was angry now. 'I wanna party; we party now.'

'I need to freshen up, sweetie. We had a long night, remember?'

'You freshen up when I tell you to freshen up, whore.' Chester's eyes were dark slits and he continued to move up the bed, over her legs now. 'I pay you to fuck me, so you fuck me. I own you!'

'Nobody owns me you fuckin' creep,' Cody snarled, and instantly regretted it.

Chester's right hand shot out and belted her across the cheek, knocking her sideways onto the bed. He was on her in a flash, straddling her and jerking her head around by the hair. She tried to fight back but for a wiry guy he was very strong. He pinned her arms down with his knees and grabbed two handfuls of her hair.

'You don't talk to me like that, you filthy fucking whore,' he shouted. He leaned down and spat in her face. 'You make me sick to my stomach that I let you fuck me. Ungrateful whore!'

He spat again then punched her in the face. Her left eye went numb and when she tried to move her head he punched it again, and again. After a couple more hits Cody couldn't open her eye anymore, so he started on the other one, before leaning down and whispering in her ear.

'I will teach you a fucking lesson, you feral whore. You will never speak to me again like this.'

And while he did his business Cody tried to block it out, but all she could think of was the fuckin' mouse eating its cheese.

6

The building near the top of Queen Street was home to a couple of non-descript Government departments involved in trade and labour. On the first five floors standard Government employees came and went, working in standard Government offices for standard pay and conditions.

Access from the sixth floor upwards was restricted to a select group of non-standard Government employees who did an exceptionally non-standard job.

Every intelligence agency in the world utilised what were known as black ops agents, whether on the payroll or as contractors. These operatives carried out the tasks that nobody ever spoke openly about but that everybody knew somehow got done. The SAS had the Counter Revolutionary Warfare Wing for special jobs; this was blacker still.

It was the sort of dirty work that kept the balance in favour of the puppet masters. Whether it was catching a diplomat el flagrante with a mistress or a whore, or organising for a foreign intelligence operative to be discovered at the airport with enough Class A drugs to guarantee a long stretch in maximum security, or recovering a wayward asset from a foreign power, there were certain people to do these certain tasks.

Or even, from time to time, eliminating a foreign asset. Assassination and dirty tricks had been part of the intelligence world since the beginning of time, and anybody who thought that the modern world, with its heightened risks and terror threats, had banished such archaic practices to the annals of history was sorely misguided. If anything, the practices had become more common. The Cold War may have been over for more than 20 years, but the War on Terror was a whole new ballgame.

And the rulebook had been re-written.

Aside from the signals espionage facilities operated by the Government Communications Security Bureau New Zealand had never been a major player in the intelligence scene, but with the opening of borders had come more pressure from international partners to get involved.

The Security Intelligence Service took most of the attention and did a good job of maintaining a bland public façade. Press releases were rare and vanilla by nature, and little was known about what they did. What was known gave the impression there was nothing worth knowing anyway.

Part of this agency officially carried the fairly non-descript title of Division 5, and operated out of the eighth floor, which was protected by the highest level of security of any floor in the building.

Its unofficial title was the Special Operations Division.

Archer arrived there at 815am and upon stepping from the elevator he was put through a metal detector, an electronic fingerprint scanner, checked for recording and transmitting devices and eventually allowed to sign in. His photo was taken by one of three plain clothed heavies and a Visitor's Pass was immediately issued.

Ingoe was summonsed and came to meet him. He wore a non-descript black suit and a striped tie, and looked equally comfortable in this as he did in DPMs.

'Thanks for coming in.'

That was the extent of the small talk as they rode the elevator up two more flights. Ingoe had never been a talker and that suited Archer; he had to admit, he felt nervous about meeting the Director.

The doors opened straight into a reception area which was lined with wooden panels and floor-to-ceiling bookcases. The shelves were full of what looked like legal tomes, and a large Persian rug adorned the polished floor in front of a PA's desk.

Behind the desk sat a trim middle-aged lady with glasses and short grey hair. She looked up from her screen and smiled. 'Morning Jed. This must be Craig?'

'It is. Craig, this is Trixie.' Ingoe waited while they shook hands. 'Trixie is the Director's PA, and knows everything about everything in the department.'

Trixie smiled warmly at him. 'You're such an old flirt, Jed,' she scolded him, 'but keep it up.' She checked her screen. 'Go on in, he's aware you're here.'

Ingoe led the way to the large panelled door to the left. He knocked twice and opened it. They entered a spacious corner office with views through tinted windows over the city on two sides. The massive oak desk facing them was almost completely clear aside from a computer screen, a phone, a coffee cup on a coaster and folded copies of the morning's Herald and Dominion.

The man crossing the floor towards them was short and slightly chubby, maybe sixty, with iron grey hair and, Archer saw as he got closer, inquisitive blue eyes. He was sharply dressed in a dark pin-striped suit and a sombre blue tie. He looked like a lecturer or a doctor.

Archer had no idea what his name was, and Ingoe had only referred to him as 'the Director.'

'Good morning, Jed.'

'Morning, sir.'

He shook Archer's hand firmly. He didn't smile, just met his gaze then stepped back and ran a quick appraising eye down the newcomer.

'Welcome.'

The Director went back behind his desk and Archer was waved to a chair across from him. Ingoe sat offline, making a triangle between the three of them with a clearly marked pecking order.

'You've had something of a distinguished career, Captain Archer,' the Director said, elbows on the arms of his chair and his eyes on Archer. 'People with credibility speak well of you...in general.'

Archer said nothing, just waited.

'Ten years in the Regular Force, Jed's old regiment Queen Alexandra's Mounted Rifles, Intelligence and the Group. You have a bent for languages and speak reasonable Arabic, Bosnian and Tetum, along with a bit of French and Russian.' The Director's eyes gave nothing away. 'Interesting mix.'

Archer nodded and waited. He already knew all this.

'It indicates to me a man with one eye on the past and one on the future. Is that right, Archer?'

'The enemies of the past don't just fade away,' Archer replied. 'If you forget the past you set yourself up to fail in the future.'

'The first man you killed was a militia fighter in East Timor. It was in a contact near the border and you were blooded at close range.'

Archer was surprised at the Director's knowledge of the incident, but tried not to show it.

'How did that feel?'

He felt the Director's gaze penetrating his head, and it made him uncomfortable. He was not used to being in the spotlight like this. He shrugged non-committally.

'We were both doing our job. It wasn't his day.'

'Do you like killing?'

Archer held the other man's gaze evenly.

'I do my job very well. If I had a problem with killing bad guys, I'd be in the wrong job.'

The Director didn't reply for several moments. Silence hung in the office. Finally, he turned his chair towards Ingoe and raised his eyebrows questioningly.

'Anything, Jed?'

Ingoe cleared his throat and sat up straighter.

'No sir. As you know, I've worked with Craig before and I have no doubt of his suitability.'

The Director nodded, contemplative now. He shifted back towards Archer and again his focus came across the desk.

'I'd like you to kidnap someone for me,' he said.

7

The elevator trip down to the basement was slow and silent. Archer mulled over what he had been told, and what had been asked of him.

It was to be an extraordinary rendition; the Government-sanctioned kidnapping of a foreign terror suspect for imprisonment and interrogation. It wasn't the first time he'd been asked to snatch someone and it wasn't the first time he'd accepted, but this time it seemed somehow different. Before it had been a part of being a Special Forces operator and almost seemed a bi-product of the actual job itself, but now it was the job.

The Director had made it clear that if the snatch itself failed, the target was to be eliminated. He also made it clear that the Brits were watching closely and were getting constant updates.

He'd now been employed as what basically amounted to a Government hitman. It wasn't soldiering and it wasn't quite spying. It was a murky grey land somewhere in the middle.

Archer had no particular moral problem with the idea. At the end of the day, he reasoned, every soldier was paid to kill for their country. But even so the whole practice had the air of unsavouriness about it.

He chided himself and discarded the thought. There was a job to be done. A bad man, a very bad man, needed to be dealt with. The sort of bad man who could only be effectively dealt with one way.

'Sometimes there's only one way,' Ingoe said, as if reading his thoughts.

Archer glanced at him and gave a self-conscious grin. The former Warrant Officer's gaze was thoughtful.

'Not having second thoughts?'

'No mate.' Archer gave a brief shake of the head. 'No second thoughts.'

Ingoe considered him for a moment as the lift came to a stop with a clunk and the doors opened.

'Good,' he said, 'because I've got some toys for you.'

They stepped into a workshop area lined with benches on one side and two full walls of shelving on the others. The smell of gun oil and leather hung in the air and Archer subconsciously inhaled deeply.

Ingoe led the way to a solid steel vault door, which he unlocked with a swipe card and a PIN code. He swung the door open to reveal a walk-in armoury and hit the lights. Archer ran his eye over the racks of weapons inside; assault rifles, sniper rifles, shotguns, sub machine guns, handguns of various makes and models.

'I could've sworn it wasn't Christmas yet,' he muttered, and Ingoe grinned wolfishly.

'You'll need a big and a small,' he said, 'and I guess probably a covert chopper.' He checked his watch. 'I'll be in the workshop, come through when you're ready and you can run them in.'

Archer walked the length of each rack, scanning the handguns and sub machine guns. It was standard for a Special Forces operative to have the flexibility to make mission-specific selections, and he had always had strong personal preferences.

He quickly found a Sig Sauer P226, the standard military sidearm, and put it to one side. It was a robust 15-shot 9mm that he'd used for years, and he knew it was reliable and accurate.

The choice for a compact sidearm was harder. He had no real

preference in this area, but knew a conservative choice would usually be best. He tossed up between another Sig, either the P229 or the P250, and the Glock 26.

He selected one of each and set them aside for now, before moving on to the sub machine guns. The Heckler and Koch MP5 was the universal choice, and he took a short K-PDW off the rack, hefting it in his hands. With a stubby barrel it unleashed a devastating 900 rounds a minute, and he'd used it before.

He took all five weapons with him through to the workshop and found Ingoe waiting with an array of holsters and magazines laid out before him on a bench. He nodded approvingly when he saw Archer's choices.

'No surprises there,' he commented, before leading the way through another heavy door into a soundproofed 35 metre shooting range.

Paper human targets hung at the far end against the bullet trap wall, and the lights were bright. An extractor fan whirred but the scent of cordite was still heavy. They stood together at a bench and loaded magazines for each of the weapons, working silently and efficiently, before both donning earmuffs and safety glasses.

When he was ready Archer moved up to the 20m mark with all five weapons and a box of magazines. Ingoe dimmed the lights a touch and observed as his new operative test fired the full size P226. A series of sets at different ranges satisfied him that it was a good selection, before Archer moved on to the three smaller pistols.

Each was put through its paces with 100 rounds being fired through it, and Ingoe's experienced eye could tell that Archer was more comfortable with the Glock than either of the Sigs. It was neither here nor there; all were excellent tools and personal preference was important. A man's familiarity with a gun was crucial when his life depended on it.

The MP5K took a 30-round magazine and Archer emptied five of them in short order, moving between targets at different ranges and raking them with short bursts of 9mm before Ingoe called a halt to proceedings.

'Now you're just showing off,' he said, cranking the lights back up.

Archer popped the empty magazine from the MP5K and double checked the chamber before putting the weapon with the others on the bench and stripping off his safety gear. He gave a satisfied grin across the bench at Ingoe.

'Haven't had a good shoot up for a while,' he commented.

Ingoe grunted. 'Best you get some practice in then,' he replied. 'You're going live in two days.'

'I'll be ready,' Archer replied, reaching for a cleaning rod.

Ingoe looked at him. 'It's a different world, sunshine,' he said. 'Just have your wits about you. It's not like the Group.'

Archer ran the rod down the barrel of the Glock. 'We're all on the same side though, aren't we?'

Ingoe gave a wolfish grin. 'Ever heard the term 'smoke and mirrors'?'

Archer cocked his head quizzically.

'What you think you see ain't always real. Magicians use smoke and mirrors to create an illusion right in front of you, so you think they're doing one thing when in fact they're doing another.' Ingoe held his gaze. 'That's what this world is all about, Archer. Get used to it fast.'

8

Archer sensed trouble as soon as he pulled into his street. He could see a dirty grey Nissan Navara ute parked in the driveway of Jazz's house, blocking in her own car. She was usually at the gym at this time of the day, so it was unusual for her to be home and he'd never seen the truck before.

He eased past her tidy little bach with the wind chimes tinkling from the apple tree out the front, buzzing down his window and cutting the radio as he did so. He didn't hear anything over the rumble of the Monaro, so turned into his driveway, stopping short of the garage and getting out.

He took his time walking to the letterbox to collect his mail, the salty breeze warm on his face and the smell of freshly mown grass all around. Seagulls swooped and squawked overhead, and a crash of breaking glass sounded from next door, followed by muffled voices.

The mail got discarded as Archer bolted across his front lawn and leaped the low side fence, arriving at the side of Jazz's place within a couple of seconds. He moved quickly and quietly along the side of the house towards the rear, the sound of an angry male voice getting louder as he got closer.

He heard Jazz's voice now, a pleading 'Please don't,' followed by the thump of heavy footsteps from the kitchen out to the small back deck.

Archer stepped into view to see a large man in a checked Swandri and jeans standing near the back door, a beer can in one hand and the other one clenched. He glanced right and saw Jazz standing just inside the door, holding a tea towel to her wrist. Her body language was submissive.

'Afternoon neighbour,' Archer called out easily, walking around the edge of the deck towards the three steps that led to the back lawn.

The other man turned and scowled at him, and a look of relief crossed Jazz's face.

'Who's this?' the other man growled at her without taking his eyes off Archer.

'I'm the neighbour,' Archer replied with a friendly smile, his hands casually tucked into his pockets. 'Craig. And you are?'

'Not interested, bud,' the man replied, and Archer quickly sized him up.

About his own height but wider in the shoulders, carrying some weight but probably very strong. Blonde curly hair and unshaven, probably mid thirties. Looked like a fisherman or labourer.

'Oh well.' Archer ignored him and glanced to Jazz, who hadn't moved. 'Just wanted to see if you're popping over for dinner later? I got some nice T-bone…'

'I said, not interested, bud.' The man moved now to the top step, chest puffed out and looking angry. From there he stood a good two feet taller than Archer. 'Take a hike.'

Archer continued to ignore him. 'I also put a nice Reisling on ice earlier, I thought…'

'Hey!' The man's tone was sharp. 'I'm talkin' to you, bud!'

'And I'm talking to the lady, so if you'd stop interrupting I'd appreciate it,' Archer replied calmly. He gave Jazz a smile, noting that the man had edged forward now and was leaning down as if to touch him. 'And did you want me to take Jojo for a run?'

'Bud!' The man's beer breath was hot and strong as he leaned down into Archer's body space. He placed his left hand on Archer's right shoulder and squeezed. 'I told you...'

Archer looked pointedly at the hand on his shoulder then up at the other man. 'And I'm telling you, friend. Take your hand off me or I'll hurt you.'

His voice was calm and quiet, but full of menace. The other man held his gaze, a pulse in his flushed neck jumping like a frog. He didn't move his hand.

'Jazz, are you okay?' Archer asked evenly, not looking at her. 'Who is this monkey?'

'Not really. This is Jason.'

'Ahh.' Archer nodded his understanding. Jazz had told him about her abusive ex-partner, enough detail for him to have taken an instant dislike to the man without ever having met him. 'That explains a lot then.'

'So you must be the soldier boy from next door,' Jason sneered, the pressure from his hand not easing. 'Take a hike, bud. This is nothing to do with you.'

'Hmm.' Archer set his jaw. 'Unfortunately, it is. So I think you need to move your hand, then get in your truck and drive away.'

Jason sneered malevolently and didn't move.

'You've got five seconds, friend,' Archer told him calmly. 'Then I'm going to move you. Understand?'

'You...'

'Five.'

'– can...'

'Four.'

'– kiss...'

'Three.'

'– my...'

'Two.'

'– hairy...'

'One.'

'– balls.'

Archer's left fist drove straight forward into Jason's crotch, smashing into his scrotum then gripping tightly and twisting. His right came up and easily swept the other man's arm away. Jason's breath exploded out in a strangled wheeze and his hands instinctively went to his groin, the beer can hitting the deck and spraying foam.

He scrabbled at Archer's hand, which remained locked tightly on his testicles.

'I told you to move,' Archer told him softly, 'you need to talk less and listen more.' He cocked his head slightly as if a thought had just occurred to him. 'Maybe that was the problem in your relationship...I don't know. But it's time for you to go now.'

Jason gasped like a landed fish, his eyes bulging. A bead of sweat was rolling down his forehead.

'Nod if you understand.'

Jason nodded.

'Now I'm going to let go, and you're going to leave. You won't come back. Are we clear?'

Jason nodded weakly again.

'First, you're going to apologise to the lady. Then you drive away. If I see you here again, I will hurt you properly. If you contact her again, I will hunt you down.' Archer's gaze was cold and flat and there was no humour or fear in his eyes. 'Understand?'

Jason managed a third weak nod.

'Good.'

Archer released his grip and Jason doubled at the waist, cupping his crotch and sucking in shallow breaths. Behind him, Jazz breathed an audible sigh and wiped her hands on the tea towel.

'Now apologise,' Archer told him.

'Fuck...'

'Don't be nasty, just apologise and go.'

'Ho..mo...ahhh.'

Jason looked up at him with anger back in his eyes, and Archer realised immediately that he was on more than beer. He straightened up and glanced back at Jazz.

'Fuckin' slut,' he spat.

Archer grabbed him by the left arm and yanked him forward, causing him to stumble down the steps onto the lawn. Jason's other hand flashed to his pocket and came out with a Stanley box cutter knife, ready to slash forwards. He started to do so, and Archer reacted instantly.

He pulled forward further, jerking Jason off balance again and side stepped at the same time, outside the knife hand. His right hand locked onto the knife hand and squeezed it closed and turned, the heel of his left hand jabbing straight and hard into Jason's right eyebrow, opening up a cut which bled immediately, then slamming it again.

He twisted the knife hand towards him, weakening the grip, and landed a left hook into his opponent's ribs, then again, and again. As Jason folded sideways Archer wrenched the knife from him and tossed it aside, pulled him downwards by the arm and gripped him by the throat. He swept Jason's legs from under him and drove him to the ground flat on his back.

There was a whoosh of air being expelled beneath his body weight as he landed on top of the other man, still holding him by the throat. Jason's face was red now and Archer eased his grip slightly, locking the bigger man's wrist under him and bracing his leg across Jason's closest knee.

The bigger man was pinned and unable to move, but the anger in his eyes had not diminished. He tried to buck, but to no avail. Archer gave his throat a squeeze.

'Don't be silly. You have three options here, *bud*.' He paused to ensure he had Jason's full attention. 'One, we lie here and wait for the cops, and you go to jail. Two, we get up, I beat the living crap out of you, then we wait for the cops and you go to jail. Or three, we get up and you drive away, never to be seen again.'

Even in his chemically-enhanced state, Jason could see he was not going to win this fight. He closed his eyes and nodded slightly. Two minutes later he was backing his ute out of the drive, his testicles throbbing and his throat aching, but with a sense of having dodged a bullet. He knew that if he ever ran into that soldier boy again, he was going to better prepared. Next time, and he promised himself there would be a next time, he would kill him.

Archer waited until the ute had disappeared from view before turning back to Jazz. She stood on the deck with her arms folded across her chest, her mouth turned down and her brow furrowed. There was sadness in her eyes.

They stared at each other for a moment before she turned and went back inside without a word.

Archer shook his head in frustration and headed home. If the silly bitch was going to be like that, she could shove it.

9

Bad-Bad Leroy had pissed and moaned alright when Cody got home.

He'd been angry that not only had she been humping her skinny ass off but worse, she'd arrived home to their shitty flat with a beat up face and a worse attitude than normal.

It took him all of sixty seconds to call her "manager" Delton, a skinny no-chest half caste Maori/Croatian bitch with a penchant for knives and his own girls. Delton rocked around in his pimped-out black Cadillac XTS, all swagger and bravado, and got the rundown from Leroy.

He checked her face like he was a goddamn doctor or some shit then held her chin in one bony hand and leaned in close. She could smell stale pot and KFC on his breath.

'Don'tchu worry, baby,' he said softly, in what she imagined he imagined was a cool, soothing tone. 'Delton knows people. Gonna get shit done, yo.'

With that he turned and walked out, snapping open his cell and hitting a speed dial button. Cody knew he had a direct line into a cop and figured that was who was on the other end. She watched him go and wondered why he always talked like he was Snoop Fuckin' Dogg.

Then Leroy started with his whinging shit again and she figured maybe talking to the cops was a better option.

Outside in the massive Caddy, Delton had the cell clamped to his ear. He waited for a few rings, inhaling the new-car smell of the Caddy. He knew the car was pretentious, he knew the fuel consumption was measured in metres per litre, and he knew it stood out like a stripper in a church, but he loved it. He'd been pulled over by more cops and had more tickets in this car than he'd had his last ten cars, but who fuckin' cared. *This shit rocked, baby.*

What Delton was concerned about right now, was that crazy-assed A-rab fuck in the hotel suite. Nobody smashed Delton's girls around but him. He hated the Five-Oh, man he fuckin' hated them, but right now he knew he needed them. Delton had gotten smarter over the years – been a time, he woulda rocked up there with his posse and popped some caps at that camel fucking biatch, but those days were gone. No way was Delton going back inside again.

The man at the other end picked up. His tone was bored and flat. 'What?'

'Cuz, we gotta sit-u-a-shun,' Delton spelled out. 'You gotta take care of it, dig?'

'Really?' The guy sounded like the veteran cop he was.

'Yeah really, yo. I'm handin' you a fuckin' ra-pist on a plate, cuz. He's got drugs and whores and shit up there; this is the career maker you been waitin' for, yo.'

'What it sounds like is a pile of bullshit to me, Delton.' The guy was on the verge of hanging up. 'I'm sicka you jerkin' me round with your "hot tips." All it ever is is you wanting me to take out one of your competitors.'

'Yeah, well,' Delton drawled, ''less you want me to let slip about you gettin' jerked off by a certain lady in my employ, you'll take this one seriously. Dig?'

10

It was midday and Yassar was still in bed, accompanied by a pair of prostitutes who had become his favourites.

Ahmed had his men in place as usual but he could tell they were all getting bored. For men hardened by war babysitting a spoilt brat while he got drunk and defiled himself was both disheartening and lacking any sort of challenge.

Ahmed himself was constantly poised, walking a wire over the hell he would face should he cock up his assignment. The Saudis were not known for their tolerance of failure. Ahmed had managed to manipulate a judge to dismiss a drink driving charge, and had paid out thousands in damages when Yassar had smashed up a hotel room in a tantrum.

The rape of the girl was certainly going to be the biggest challenge, and he was struggling to see how it could be made to go away. This was not Australia; corruption was low and it was very difficult to manage such situations.

The patriarch of the family, Yassar's Sheikh father, had been made aware immediately and a plan was in place to deal with the situation, but Yassar was not going to like it. Ahmed was waiting on a phone call to be made this afternoon from the Sheikh himself, informing Yassar of the plan. He had warned his team to be ready for the biggest tantrum yet.

As he stood watching the traffic below, his phone buzzed and he tapped the Bluetooth. It was Kholini, one of the senior men in the Sheikh's security detail and Ahmed's immediate boss. As the other man made his greetings, Ahmed observed a pair of cars pull up below and double park half on the footpath. They were both unmarked Holden Commodores, which he knew were standard Police cars, and the four people – three men, one woman – looked every inch Police in their off-the-rack suits and sensible shoes.

One of the men hitched his belt at the right hip, a sure giveaway that he was armed. The four officers walked determinedly towards the entrance to the hotel below him.

Kholini spoke with a calm urgency. A phone call had been made and the Police were on the way.

Ahmed nodded to himself. 'I see them,' he said, 'they have just arrived.'

Kholini continued to speak and Ahmed listened without interrupting. The plan was being brought forward, with some necessary tweaking, and he had thirty minutes to complete his end of it.

'No problem,' Ahmed replied confidently. 'He will be there. I will see to it.'

'And the other part?' Kholini queried. 'We need maximum exposure, Ahmed. This must be all over the media tomorrow. Understand?'

'I understand. I'll be in touch.'

Kholini disconnected and Ahmed immediately keyed his walkie talkie, calling his men to him. They only had a couple of minutes to act. Kamal and Dhara were brothers, Saudi Arabian Army veterans of the first Gulf War. They were battle hardened and ruthless, and had worked with him as a Close Protection Team for several years now.

'The Police are coming,' he told them. 'They are here to arrest our principal. There are four of them and they are armed.'

He glanced at each man in turn. Kamal was the older of the two, with a heavy moustache. Dhara was the slicker brother, with styled hair and a Don Johnson-style stubble – or George Michael, as Kamal liked to tease him.

'They are to be taken out. They will not take our principal. I will move him, you deal with the Police. Are we clear?'

Both men nodded without question and paused to bump fists before moving.

11

Archer had arrived early at HQ to beat the traffic.

The day started with handing over the Monaro keys to a whiz-kid techo who looked about twelve, then being escorted upstairs by Ingoe for more briefings.

As they waited for the lift a forest green Holden Colorado rolled past, heading for the exit. The driver was a big unit, well over six foot and very broad, a rugged looking character in his late twenties. Archer did a double take as they made eye contact, and the other man gave him a brief tilt of the chin in acknowledgement.

Archer couldn't recall his name but recognised him as a cop, a member of the Special Tactics Group that he'd trained with before. The STG were the Police SWAT-style unit, nicknamed the "Super Tough Guys." Ingoe gave the other man a nod as the wagon went past, and glanced at Archer.

'Yes,' he said in answer to the unasked question. 'One of us.'

Archer raised his eyebrows. 'How many?'

Ingoe smiled faintly. 'Enough. You'll get to meet them all in due course, they just don't tend to be around at the same time.'

Most of the morning was spent being briefed by Ingoe in more detail on his mission, and then being issued with more kit. He was the proud owner of a new iPhone, laptop and identity card.

New ID documents complete with legend would be ready the next day, Ingoe told him. He was to take the Glock 26 with him and report to the Group's Killing House at Ardmore the next day for a training session with a couple of other specialists.

They were done by lunchtime and Ingoe escorted him back downstairs. They crossed the garage to a work bay where a couple of technicians were at work on the Monaro. Archer watched in silence as they finished installing a state-of-the-art alarm system to help protect the other couple of bits of wizardry they'd already put in. His mind drifted to the mission.

The target was protected by an expert CP team, all armed, and ensconced in the Presidential suite of one of the top hotels in the city. He needed to be snatched subtly, and it was up to Archer to decide how. He had three restrictions; no publicity, no collateral damage, and only four days to do it.

A surveillance team had been on him round the clock for the last week so working out a pattern was easy. Archer already had the bones of a plan in his head; he just needed to get the lay of the land for himself so he could flesh it out. He knew the best way to impress the Director – and Ingoe, for that matter – would be to get the job done quickly and quietly, ahead of schedule.

The cops had intel that he was smashed on drugs and using hookers almost constantly, both factors which threw up fish hooks to be managed. The Special Investigations Group, the spooks' contact point in the cops, was closely monitoring the activities but were unaware of the planned rendition.

Archer had no interest in the inter-departmental politics and was working out a timeline when Ingoe's phone rang and he stepped aside to answer it.

A frown creased his face and he looked up at Archer, jabbing an urgent finger at the Monaro. Archer was moving already as the former RSM disconnected. The technicians jumped back as Ingoe barked orders.

'Our guy at SIG just called. The cops're going there now to arrest him for raping some girl. They're out of their depth; his team won't let him be taken. SIG're trying to get it stalled but no dice so far.'

Archer opened the small satchel he was carrying and removed the Glock, slapping a mag into it and racking the slide. He clipped a hip holster onto his belt and secured the weapon, tucking a second magazine into his pocket and tossing the satchel onto the passenger's seat as he fired up the Monaro, the throaty roar filling the basement garage. He eased back out of the work bay, buzzing the window down and killing the stereo. One of the techs ran to open the exit gate.

Ingoe put a hand on the windowsill and walked beside him as he manoeuvred out of the tight space. 'We're trying to get hold of the cops and will get back up there as quickly as we can. You need to intercept the cops before they get in the door.'

'I'm on it.' Archer paused long enough to buckle up then slipped it into gear.

Ingoe stepped back from the window now. 'There'll be a bloodbath – get up there and stop it!'

The tyres squealed on the concrete and the Monaro jumped forward like a horny jackrabbit.

12

Ahmed walked straight to the master bedroom door and pushed it open.

One of the whores was snapping photos of the other posing with Yassar on the bed. All three were completely naked, and an empty Bollinger bottle lay on the floor.

Yassar glared at him as he entered. Neither of the women made any attempt to hide their nakedness from the bodyguard; it wasn't like he hadn't seen it before.

'What do you think this is?' Yassar demanded, dragging a silk pillow over his crotch. 'Get out!'

'The Police are here. We are leaving.' Ahmed paused. Nobody moved. 'Now!'

'Who the fuck...' The photographer started to speak but stopped when Ahmed turned to her.

'Stop talking,' he said coldly, stalking to the bed. He jabbed a finger at the other whore. 'Move!'

Yassar tried to muster himself, but they could all see it was in vain. Ahmed snatched a pair of trousers off the floor and threw them to him.

'Your father's orders,' he said simply.

It was enough. Yassar began to struggle into his pants, both whores standing back to watch silently. Loud voices sounded at the foyer, followed by a burst of gunfire. One of the whores shrieked and Yassar looked up in alarm.

Ahmed remained impassive, trusting his men to deal with the problem. He waited until Yassar had pulled on his shirt, handed him a pair of shoes, and ushered him towards the door. More shooting sounded, a mix of a sub machine gun and pistols, accompanied by a scream and thudding.

As the two men pushed through the bedroom doors, one of the prostitutes spoke up.

'What about us? What the fuck, man?'

Ahmed stopped in the doorway and drew his weapon. It was a Ruger P89 he had strapped to his hip every minute of the day. He turned and brought the gun up. One of the whores screamed, the scream cut short when Ahmed dropped her with a double tap to the chest. The second one froze on the bed, too scared to move. Ahmed double tapped her too before turning away and hustling Yassar along with him.

Yassar dismissed the incident as quickly as it had happened. Life was cheap in his world and a pair of prostitutes meant nothing.

They heard a longer burst of fire followed by running feet, another burst and a thump.

'Clear,' Kamal shouted.

Ahmed led Yassar into the foyer, where they were joined by Kamal, who had a Mini Uzi in his hands. Two policemen lay on the floor outside the door, their chests ripped open by rounds. Neither even had their weapons drawn.

Dhara lay face down near the elevator doors, which were jammed open on a woman's leg. Blood flowed steadily from his head. Ahmed glanced inquisitively at Kamal, who shrugged.

'One of them hung back, and got him,' he said simply. 'I took care of them.'

'Good.' Ahmed nodded and moved to the stairs. 'We must go.'

'I will clear the way.' Kamal led the way and opened the door. He entered the stairwell and was back a moment later. 'It is clear. I hear shouting though.' His dark eyes glittered with excitement. 'More Police will be here soon.'

'No problem.' Ahmed nodded and ushered his principal through the door, before pausing and turning back to his comrade. 'One more thing.'

Kamal waited expectantly, and Ahmed shot him in the face at point blank range. Blood and brain matter sprayed the wall across the foyer and Kamal's body dropped in a heap.

Ahmed paused for a moment. He had fought alongside Kamal for several years now and they were closer than brothers. But orders were orders.

He turned and saw Yassar watching him, a sick look on his face. Ahmed switched back to the task.

'Let's go.'

13

Yassar crossed the foyer of the Landon and made for the front doors. His black Lexus pulled up as he reached the doors, and the concierge opened his door for him as he reached the car.

Giving the liveried man a curt nod, Yassar slipped into the backseat and caught Ahmed's glance in the rear view mirror. He gave Ahmed an inquisitive look.

Ahmed nodded abruptly. 'Still there,' the older man said.

Yassar let out a sigh of frustration and rubbed a hand over his face.

'Why me?' he whined. 'Why this?' He bumped his forehead against the seat back in front of him and let out a groan. 'It's all such a mess.'

Ahmed studied him in the rear view mirror. On the way down the stairs he had filled him in on the plan. Yassar didn't like it, but being who he was meant this was not the first time such drastic measures had been taken. He had given Ahmed his agreement, as if it mattered, and had quickly got his head in the game.

'Don't worry,' Ahmed said coolly, 'they are fools. If we move fast and decisively, we will make our rendezvous. We will go.'

Yassar flopped back in his seat and Ahmed moved smoothly round the hotel to the exit, indicating correctly and within moments was merging onto Symonds Street. Traffic was light and he headed north towards the city centre, constantly checking his mirrors.

'Silver Mazda, three back,' he said, 'dark blue Subaru, inside lane.'

Yassar sighed again and squeezed the bridge of his nose. His head was throbbing.

'Lose them,' he said quietly. 'I'm sick of these fools.'

Ahmed's look in the mirror was questioning. He knew what such an overt move would mean.

'Lose them,' Yassar snapped. 'Now!'

Ahmed accelerated smoothly, cutting inside the car in front and causing it to brake hard as he swerved back. He saw the silver Mazda immediately try to catch up but its progress was stalled by the people mover he'd just cut off.

He allowed himself a smile and gassed it again, hitting eighty as he flew down Symonds Street. The silver Mazda fell out of view as he turned right onto Grafton Street and he felt a buzz of satisfaction.

Suddenly he caught a flash of movement behind him and looked up sharply, seeing the blue Subaru flying up behind him.

Ahmed scowled to himself and put his foot down, but the Subaru had serious grunt and bolted after him. Ahmed switched to Plan B, and slammed on the brakes. Yassar was thrown forward with a curse and the Subaru driver reacted too late, overshooting before he realised and skidded to a halt twenty metres ahead. Ahmed moved forward and collided with the front left wing of the Subaru, shunting the surveillance car sideways across the centreline.

He floored it and rammed the Subaru into a station wagon that had stopped in its lane then steered away and accelerated again, leaving the Subaru behind.

In his rear view mirror he saw the silver Mazda racing after him, overtaking traffic on the outside and approaching the wrecked Subaru.

For the second time Ahmed skidded to a halt, snatching his own

Mini Uzi from under the driver's seat and jumping out. The Mazda was going way too fast to stop in time now and Ahmed stood in the middle of Grafton Rd, bracing the stubby submachine gun with both hands as he snapped off short bursts.

Sparks flew from the body of the Mazda and he saw the windscreen shatter. The driver locked up and went into a skid, still swerving to try and hit him. Ahmed back pedalled, only a couple of metres from the Mazda as it came past him.

He pinned the trigger back and hosed the last fifteen rounds along the passenger's side, blowing out the windows.

The Mazda went airborne and rolled a complete 360, smashed into an oncoming light truck and flipped again before skidding on its roof into the kerb and flipping onto its side on the footpath. Ahmed tossed the Mini Uzi back into the Lexus and hit the gas.

Archer raced up the outside of the traffic, ignoring the blast of horns and swerving left to avoid a head-on with an Indian taxi driver as he accelerated heavily along Wellesley Street. He felt a clip on his rear wing as he cut too close to a car but carried on, overtaking again and making ground. A hefty Suzuki 1100 motorbike carrying a surveillance officer was rapidly catching up behind him.

He saw a head appear from the left rear passenger's window, followed by an arm and a flash. A second flash came and Archer accelerated harder. The shooter had to be Yassar himself, and he was confident the financier was no marksman.

The head disappeared and the black Lexus leaped forward again, slipping right over the centreline and driving straight at the oncoming traffic. Cars swerved and immediately there was a pile up, one car sideswiping another as it took evasive action, another running up the back of both of them as they braked hard.

Archer cut up the inside of a courier van and crushed the pedal down, surging after the Lexus with the engine starting to growl as they merged onto the northbound motorway.

Ahmed hung wide, cutting across both lanes as he merged at over 100. He got into the outside lane and gunned it.

The red Monaro was flying behind him, slipping between the

inside and centre lanes to avoid a collision as Archer smoothly worked the transmission and goosed the accelerator.

A light delivery truck was hogging the outside lane and Ahmed drifted left, clipping the front panel of a hatchback as he did so. The hatch went into a spin behind him, directly in front of the Monaro, and Ahmed allowed himself a tight smile.

Archer stabbed the brake pedal down and dropped the gears, jaw set with determination, and slipped left, missing the spinning hatchback by a hair's breadth then gunning it hard as he swung wide again to get into the outside lane.

Yassar leaned out of the right rear window now, a pistol in his hand flashing as he pumped the trigger. His aim was better now and Archer was closer. The first round went wide but the second skipped off the Monaro's bonnet, causing Archer to flinch without losing speed.

He cursed and accelerated under a third round, seeing the Suzuki biker haring up on the left. Too eager, he thought, and sure enough a couple of seconds later Yassar was jabbing his pistol out the left rear window.

A shot flashed out and the biker swerved, over-corrected and lost control. The bike tipped right and the rider spilled into the middle lane, landing heavily as his bike skidded in a spray of sparks.

Archer hung right on the approach to the Harbour Bridge, seeing the Lexus veer left across the motorway into the left lane. He dodged a family wagon and a motorcyclist and followed it, a suspicion forming in his mind as he thumped across the dividing strips. The harbour stretched out below them, blue and sparkling, dotted with small boats and a couple of wave runners.

The Lexus raced up the bridge, sideswiping a taxi and pushing it into the median barrier, and as it neared the crest, the brake lights suddenly flared and it skidded to a halt, slewing across the lane.

Archer was still several lengths back and pumped his own brakes, slowing rapidly at the same time as the driver's door and right rear door flew open on the far side of the Lexus. Both men alighted and took cover behind the car.

He jerked the handbrake on and snapped the steering wheel to the right, skidding to a halt side on across the lane. A burst of automatic fire sounded and the passenger's window exploded inwards as Archer dived out onto the road, drawing his own weapon as he did so. He rolled behind the rear wheel, more shots impacting on the car body, and sneaked a peek underneath. He could see a pair of feet beneath the other car just a few metres away and quickly lined up his front sight. He snapped off a double tap from the Glock, seeing the left foot kick out and the knee above it hit the ground, a scream sounding across the gap.

He squeezed another double tap, the leg jerking with the impacts, but still the guy didn't fall.

Archer moved to the rear wing of his car and threw a quick look around, just in time to see Yassar moving. Archer started to move too but saw the second guy appear over the boot of the Lexus, a machine pistol in his hands. A stream of rounds blasted the back of the Monaro and sprayed Archer with glass shards before he got down again. He sneaked a quick peek and saw Yassar had climbed onto the railing of the bridge, a cell phone in his hand. He was facing out towards the harbour, the phone to his ear.

'Don't move, Yassar!' Archer bellowed, aiming across the boot at him.

The other man glanced back at him and smiled cockily.

'You'll never take me, you filthy capitalist pig,' he sneered, and tossed the phone out into the blue.

A split second later he followed it, stepping out and dropping from sight. Archer was up and running, checking the Lexus as he did so. The driver with the chopper rose awkwardly, the Uzi's barrel coming round. Archer pumped two shots at him, the first punching him straight in the chest and the second taking a chunk of his temple off as he fell backwards.

Cars were jammed up all around, civilians staring in amazement at the carnage on the bridge. He could see several holding up cell phones to film the action.

Archer leaned over the rail and saw Yassar hit the water in a plume of spray. The two wave runners he'd seen earlier were racing towards him, and it was clear to Archer that this was all planned. A high-risk, high-profile escape. Daring and exciting. Front page news and an inspiration to the faithful followers around the world.

He yanked his jacket off and tossed it aside, jumping up onto the railing. The wave runners were closing in down below and he saw Yassar's head break the surface.

Archer holstered his weapon and took a deep breath then jumped, folding his arms up across his chest and keeping his knees together.

Just like freefall training.

14
———

The blue surface rushed up and suddenly he hit it, plunging deep and throwing his arms and legs out to slow his descent.

The water was like a cold slap, and he felt the current immediately tug at his body. He kicked hard, pushing up and craning his neck to see as he did so. Getting closer to the surface he saw the two wave runners floating there, a blur of movement and then zipping lines of bubbles as bullets flew into the water a few metres away from him.

Archer tugged his Glock free and extended it as he surged upwards, triggering a couple of shots as one of the wave runners raced away in a cloud of bubbles and white froth.

His head burst into the open just a metre from the second wave runner, and the rider swung towards him, the ugly snout of an Ingram MAC-10 following his gaze. Archer brought the Glock up and snapped out the last two shots, catching the rider first in the throat then the upper lip, throwing him backwards off the runner in a cloud of red, the sub machine gun loosing off a burst of rounds at the sky.

Archer struck out for the runner and hauled himself on from the rear, sucking in air as he watched the gunman roll onto his front and float away. He dropped the magazine and did a speed change, chambered a fresh round and re-holstered the weapon.

The other wave runner was nearly fifty metres away, heading towards open water, Yassar clinging to the rider. He was watching over his shoulder and Archer saw him lean forward to warn the rider.

Archer gunned the wave runner after them, ducking low and opening it up in a desperate bid to catch them. The surface was rippled with a light wind and the wave runner bounced across the top, spray kicking up around it with every slap down. The wind whipped at his wet clothes and Archer cleared the drips from his face with a quick wipe. He settled in for the ride, scanning about for other threats as he raced across the harbour, but didn't see any.

They were motoring past other boats, mostly pleasure craft with fishing lines in the water. He glimpsed a girl sunbathing topless on the deck of a substantial cruiser as he flew by, large sunglasses shielding her eyes as she lazily watched him pass, making no effort to cover herself.

Archer turned back to the chase and focussed on the back of the escaping terrorist.

Unburdened by the weight of a passenger, he was gaining ground as they left the harbour and reached the open sea, and he began to plan his tactics on how to affect the capture.

Suddenly the wave runner in front of him cut power and spun in a tight turn, circling to confront the pursuer. Archer eased off on the throttle and waited to see how they were going to proceed.

The rider swung a MAC-10 forward on its sling from under his arm, answering the question with a burst of fire. There was a 30-metre gap between them, and the wave runner was an unstable platform, allowing the burst to go high.

Archer snatched the Glock from his hip and triggered a snap shot before gunning the runner away to the right. Even though the stubby sub machine gun had a very limited effective range, it carried a 30-round magazine against his compact pistol, and he had no desire to engage in a close quarter battle out here.

He turned again, seeing the other rider bringing the SMG up to eye level, trying to aim as best he could. Archer snapped another shot, firing one handed, and got close enough to make the gunner flinch and involuntarily jerk his barrel wide, wasting a good burst of ammo.

Archer moved again, cutting a tight circle and throwing up a curtain of water as concealment. The throb of rotors reached his ears and he saw the Police heli approaching from Mechanics Bay.

At the same time, he saw a lavish yacht ploughing towards them from the opposite direction.

The other rider unleashed another burst, a line of bullets skipping across the water in front of Archer's wave runner, and he threw a shot back to dissuade anything further. The rider raised the MAC-10 and emptied the magazine at him, hosing a spray of lead that sliced the air millimetres above Archer's head.

Archer threw his weight sideways, tucking in tight to the chassis of the runner and letting it right itself as he clung to it, watching the other runner turn and accelerate away. The Police heli was skimming low as it got closer, and he turned his attention to the large yacht as it also approached.

A man on the bow was raising a tube to his shoulder, and turned it towards the heli.

Archer cursed and waved desperately at the heli, vainly trying to warn them off as the man with the RPG settled his sights. A rocket propelled grenade flashed forward and up, a smoke trail marking its path across the sky as it zeroed in on the heli. The pilot reacted at the last second and banked hard, the rocket whooshing past in a narrow miss.

The heli continued its evasive manoeuvre by pulling right back, ducking and weaving as it made its way to a safe distance. The gunner on the deck turned his attention towards Archer, slipping a second rocket into the tube.

The first wave runner was nearly at the yacht now and Archer cursed, cranked the throttle and leaped it forward, the nose lifting at the same time as he saw the gunner settling into his aim.

He snarled another curse and raised the Glock, emptying the

magazine wildly in the gunner's direction but to no avail. He saw the rocket launch and he dived right, plunging into the water a second before the wave runner exploded in a ball of flame, sending chunks of hot steel sizzling in all directions.

Archer felt a tug as a piece of shrapnel ripped across his left side and he clapped a hand to it, gasping for air as he surfaced. The yacht slowed enough to take aboard the two new passengers before turning in a wide circle around Archer as he bobbed helplessly in the tide, powerless to stop them.

Yassar came to the side rail and threw a rude gesture at him as the yacht powered away, an arrogant sneer on his face as he laughed at his opponent.

'Better luck next time,' he jeered.

Archer swore angrily and watched the yacht disappear out to sea.

15

The Service doctor had patched the wound on Archer's hip and sent him on his way with clear instructions on wound care.

Archer hardly listened; partly because he was a trained medic anyway, but mostly because he was so angry with himself. He'd let his target get away on his first mission, there was a (fortunately) grainy photo from somebody's cell phone of him at the centre of a media frenzy, and he'd received an immediate 'forthwith' to the Director's office.

As soon as he shut the office door Archer felt the wrath of the man.

'I thought you were supposed to be a bloody professional, Archer,' the Director told him coldly. 'All I've seen so far is amateur hour, and my balls are in a sling because of it.'

Archer stood stiffly in front of the desk, fixing his gaze on a painting on the wall opposite. It was a dark oil painting of some kind of old-fashioned English countryside scene with an effeminate-looking shepherd boy and his dog. Archer had never followed art at all and had no idea whether it was an original or a print. It didn't matter much right now, as long as it kept his focus from the Director's icy gaze.

'The last thing we needed was to have this plastered all over the media, but that's what I now have to deal with – and what I have to try and explain to the PM.'

The Director wasn't a pacer; he sat perfectly still behind his desk, hands flat on the surface. Somehow his physical calmness made the fury in his words more noticeable, and Archer suddenly felt very isolated and vulnerable.

'I gave you three rules for this mission; no publicity, no collateral and four days to do it in. You've got us on the breaking news with a trail of wrecked cars and bullet casings behind you.'

'In a timely fashion though, sir.' Archer's attempt at levity was poorly timed. The Director's expression told him that a fresh turd on his dinner plate would have been more welcome.

'This agency has made an excellent name for itself and in one fell swoop that's been torn down by one man's inability to carry out a simple task. Any fool could've embarrassed the Government like this.'

Archer bristled at the jibe, and the Director picked up on it immediately.

'Did you have something to say in your defence, Archer?' he inquired. 'I'd love to hear it.'

Archer stopped staring at the effeminate shepherd boy and looked at the other man.

'You have a leak,' he said flatly.

It was the Director's turn to bristle and his nostrils flared. He pursed his lips and fixed Archer with a withering look.

'And what the hell gives you licence to make accusations like that?' he snapped. 'You've got a bloody cheek!'

'Well how the hell did that debacle happen then?' Archer snapped back. 'Those cops were gunned down in the elevator – they were ambushed. Yassar had help to get out of there, and if the details were kept so secure then it shouldn't be too hard to find out who talked.'

'You watch your tongue.'

'And you watch your back.'

The Director stood now and glared across the desk at him. Archer glared straight back and for several moments neither man backed down.

'You're an arrogant son of a bitch,' the Director said frostily. 'You think I don't realise that? I've been living in the shadows since you were jerking off to Commando comics son, so don't come in here shouting the odds and stating the obvious. You've spent your adult life as a blunt instrument, a sledgehammer for cracking nuts, but you're in a different world now. It's a world of shadow dancers and half truths, where more often than not the easy way is the wrong way, where you don't trust your enemies and you certainly don't trust your friends. Nothing is what it seems until you've triple-confirmed it, and every move we make is calculated for a purpose. Our actions can bring down Governments, so we don't have the luxury of a practice run.'

The Director paused to let that sink in.

'People told me you were the right man for the job, but it appears they may have been wrong. Were they wrong, Archer?'

Archer took a slow breath and rolled his jaw to ease the tension before speaking.

'No sir,' he replied softly, 'they weren't wrong.'

The Director considered him for a long moment, as if mulling over his decision.

'I sincerely hope not. But for now, the mission is not over. Get out there and finish it.' He paused before continuing. 'And if you get it wrong again, I'll have your bloody guts for garters.'

16

The light plane landed at 10pm, and Yassar was hustled into a blue Toyota Surf with blacked out windows. Not that anyone was paying attention anyway; money had changed hands and that was that.

The driver of the Surf was a tall Samoan who introduced himself as Afa. He moved with the lean smoothness of an athlete and had a pistol tucked into the waistband of his ragged jeans. His partner was shorter and stockier and had the shoulders and arms of a power lifter.

He didn't bother to introduce himself, just roughly frisked Yassar and put him in the backseat.

Afa drove and Yassar switched off, letting tiredness take over as the Surf hummed through Apia city centre and into the mountains. He had no idea where they were and it occurred to him that, if it all went south, he would be in a very sticky situation indeed. But he was anyway, so what did it matter? He closed his eyes and leaned against the window.

It had been a frantic day and a half-the yacht had been met at sea by a chopper which winched Yassar up like a worm on a fishing line, flew him back to a private landing strip in Northland, and transferred him to a light plane. They had flown to Sydney first then somewhere in the remote Northern Territories, and on from there on the last leg.

It seemed like only seconds later that the Surf slowed and turned off onto a bumpy road, rolling and dipping a good couple of hundred metres through a tree lined avenue until they burst forth onto a wide expanse of open land.

The headlights swept across the facade of a wide house as the Surf turned and parked at the front door. The building looked like something from days gone by, like the mansion of a Georgia plantation owner in the days of slavery and cotton picking, big wooden shutters and an expansive porch with a rocking chair and swing seat.

A man was silhouetted by the light spilling out the open front door. Average height and long in the body, short stocky legs, and curly auburn hair. As Yassar took the steps to the porch the man extended his hand and broke into a broad smile.

'Hello my friend,' Yassar enthused, reaching out to pump the other man's hand. Boyle's grip was strong but brief, and Yassar got the first inkling that things were not quite going to go as he'd planned. 'It is so good to see you again.'

Boyle nodded and gave a non-committal grunt as he released the hand shake. He appraised the newcomer silently. 'Ye're in a spot of bother, wee man.'

Yassar's smile faltered and he shifted his feet uncomfortably. 'I guess you could say that...' He turned and waved an arm at their surroundings. 'What a paradise, I must say, hey? Beautiful.' He clasped his hands together and shook his head, gazing with admiration at the Irishman. 'Absolutely beautiful.'

'Don't suck my dick, pal,' Boyle said softly, the tiniest hint of a smile playing at his lips. 'This is business. We have a lot to talk about.'

Yassar's smile faltered further. Things were most definitely not going to plan, he reflected. Still, perhaps he could talk his way through this and come out the other side. After all, he was Yassar, he was Saudi royalty. No Irish village-idiot was going to outsmart him.

But despite his bravado, as he stepped across the threshold into the old house, Yassar couldn't help feeling he was passing the point of no return.

17

Air New Zealand's NZ2 flight landed at London Heathrow at 1:45pm.

On this Wednesday among its passengers was Craig Archer, a management consultant who was travelling alone and on his own passport. He joined the throng at one of the busiest airports in the world, shuffling to collect his luggage then jostling for position to get through Immigration as quickly as possible.

The Immigration officer paid him no particular attention, but Archer was certain he was being watched. His background and previous travels would have ensured he was on the international watch-list, even before the Service had organised the visit and notified their British counterparts of his impending arrival.

He'd left Auckland twenty eight hours ago, transited Los Angeles for five hours, and spent the entire flight sat next to a muscular young Indian man who smelled of curry and wore far too much hair product. He also noted with a sneer the paperback that the guy was reading. It was one of a plethora purportedly written by an ex-Regiment soldier who had left under a cloud and publicly touted himself as a hero. Archer had met him once and the guy lived in a fantastic parallel universe. His bestsellers were ghost written and Archer refused to read him on principle.

He'd done plenty of covert trips overseas before and rarely had issues with security services, but he had a feeling time would be different. Sure enough, in the Arrivals hall of Terminal Four he spotted a watcher lurking near the door, a sporty looking young black guy with ear buds in and a carry bag over his shoulder. He ignored him and stopped to buy a bottle of water before joining the queue for a cab, waiting seven minutes before climbing into a black cab and giving the driver the name of his hotel in Marble Arch.

He settled back for the journey, not even bothering to check his tail for the watchers he knew would be there, but instead happily reflecting that on most previous trips to London he'd either been picked up by a mate or caught the tube into Victoria.

The joys of travelling on the Government's ticket, he thought.

Twenty five minutes later the cab pulled up at the kerb and Archer handed over his credit card, added on the appropriate tip – against his natural instincts – and carried his own luggage into Reception.

The girl at the front desk was Eastern European – probably Polish, he guessed – and checked him in with minimal fuss and even less personality. Archer didn't care-all he wanted was a drink, a shower and a warm bed. The meal onboard had been sufficient and he had slept briefly.

He took the lift to the third floor, noted that the neighbouring rooms were silent, and as soon as he unlocked the door he detected the presence of someone in the darkened room. His senses went instantly to full alert.

He stepped to the side and was about to slip the access card into the power slot, when the other person spoke.

'Calm down Arch, it's just me.' Then, almost as an afterthought, 'Oh, and *Han Solo*.'

It was a man's voice, calm and with a touch of amusement, and it came from the armchair by the window.

'*Millennium Falcon*,' Archer replied, wondering who the hell came up with these ridiculous code words. He hit the lights and immediately recognised the man sitting watching him, a glass of beer in one hand. His face split into a grin and he crossed the floor to shake hands.

Rob Moore had served the last 15 years of his 20-year military career in Special Forces before retiring and dropping out of sight. He'd been an exemplary soldier, and had been a troop Sergeant in Mountain Troop when Archer had taken over as the OC. The experienced NCO had taught him many things and eased him into life in the Group.

He was a huskily built man with greying temples and a weathered complexion, dressed casually in jeans and a brown leather bomber jacket.

'You haven't changed a bit,' Moore told him with a grin, pumping his hand in a ferocious grip, 'put on a bit of weight though, boy.'

'Funny, you just look older.' Archer smiled warmly and dropped his overnighter on the bed. 'Still having to work, then?'

Moore slapped him on the arm and sat down again. He gestured towards the fridge of the standard studio room.

'Help yourself to a drink,' he said graciously, 'it's on the firm.'

Archer nodded and shed his jacket, pouring himself a bourbon and cola in a tumbler, aware of Moore watching him throughout.

'So, we're clean here?' he asked, whirling a finger at the ceiling and walls.

'As we'll ever be,' Moore replied, taking a draught of his beer. 'So obviously I'm your welcoming committee, and I'll be here in the morning to take you to your meeting across the bridge.'

'So this is where you got to then.'

Moore inclined his head.

'After an apprenticeship elsewhere. Been here a while now though.' He shrugged. 'I like it, suits me. I get to travel to exotic places, meet interesting people...'

'And we know the rest,' Archer finished for him. 'So we share an employer again?'

'We do.' Moore gave a short nod and drained his glass. He stood and put the glass on the counter top. 'I'll pick you up at nine. I'd say you'll be done by eleven.'

He moved towards the door then paused. 'Oh, and the full English here is crap. Best off getting something elsewhere.' He opened the door and winked. 'Sleep tight, Chucklehead.'

Archer locked the door behind him and sipped his drink as he stood at the window, watching Moore cross the road below and disappear up the street.

The former NCO was a throwback to his previous life, and the surest sign yet of the new life he'd now entered. Like anyone in his world he'd always suspected roles like this had existed-hell, some nations made no secret about it-but aside from the odd whisper he'd never had anything to base his suspicions on. Seeing Moore, and knowing his background, cemented it for him that this new life was not a fantasy at all, it was a stone cold reality.

Archer felt a thrill run through him as he contemplated what lay ahead of him. He had never been interested in the hum-drum existence of everyday life, of commuting to a generic office in a beige Toyota and coming home to a mousey wife and a picket fence. Such a thought chilled him and he knew, without a shadow of a doubt, that if he were forced into such an existence, he would certainly wilt and die.

He lived for action and adventure, the buzz of life on the edge, of pitting himself against the odds and battling to win, whether it was scaling a rain-slick mountainside, penetrating defences to obtain intelligence or plant a bomb, or engaging the enemy at close quarters in one of the world's hellholes.

Challenges like that were the foods of life for men like Archer and Moore. Just as certainly as his military career had come to an end, the chapter of being on the circuit had closed, and now a new chapter of adventure awaited him.

Archer drained his glass and set it down before stripping off and taking a short cold shower. The pressure was hard and he was soon revived. He changed into jeans and a warm outdoors jacket before hitting the street to find a meal.

He took a window seat in a nearby pizza place and people watched as he ate. The Spanish waitress had firm, pert breasts and legs made for wrapping around a man. She showed some interest and he debated hard about taking it further. He was still annoyed about how things had ended with Jazz, who had studiously avoided him since the run in with her ex, and the urge to be with a woman was strong. Nobody need know. He finally decided against it, knowing that after the debacle in Auckland any further hiccups would not be treated lightly.

He downed his Peroni and left a ten quid tip instead, making his way back to the hotel where he took a long hot soak to wash away the fug of 28 hours of international travel. The heat and alcohol helped tiredness to descend suddenly, and he hit the sack, pleased the bed was firm and warm.

Within seconds he was in a deep and dreamless sleep.

18

He woke at 5am, wide awake and feeling like he'd slept all day.

He threw on gym gear and took a jog through Hyde Park, a light rain falling and his breath steaming as he worked out the kinks and got the blood pumping. He loved London any time of year, and had never understood people who moaned about the weather and the rush and the overcrowding. It was one of the most interesting cities in the world as far as Archer was concerned, and he envied Moore getting a posting here.

If all went well and he had some time to spare before flying home, he intended to head to Charing Cross Road and browse the old bookshops, eat at Covent Garden and share a couple of pints with Moore at a Weatherspoon's – any Weatherspoon's. He'd last been here a year ago and spent an enjoyable long weekend with a Qantas air hostess, eating drinking and making love in a West End hotel.

Archer exited the park and glanced back as he did so, catching sight of the jogger he'd seen earlier. A pair of white men in their thirties, label gear and not talking, keeping pace with him from a hundred yards or so back. They had matching short back and sides haircuts and looked like gym bunnies.

American, he thought to himself, *probably feds*.

He wondered why they were keeping tabs on him, but more so, wondered how good they were.

Picking up the pace, he turned right out of the park onto Bayswater Rd and headed towards the hotel. He knew they would have seen him lift the pace and would presumably do likewise. Glancing around, he couldn't see a spotter in sight.

Archer quickly turned and retraced his steps. It was one of the oldest tricks in the book.

As he rounded the hedge that bordered the entrance path, he heard the two sets of approaching footfalls hurrying towards him.

He raced around the corner and crashed straight into them, bringing his elbow up into the solar plexus of the closest one and knocking the wind out of him. He grabbed the second guy's sweater and they all tumbled to the ground in a tangle of arms and legs.

In the confusion Archer managed to keep the first guy beneath him and rode him to the ground, slamming him flat on his back and double-winding him. The other guy reacted quickly and broke free, rolling away and getting to his feet in a tae kwon do stance.

Archer rolled off the first guy, who was gasping for breath and scrabbling at the wet ground, and glanced up at the second guy. Even two years later, on a rainy London morning, he recognised the man.

He was the team leader whose gunner had killed Bula on the Highway to Hell.

'You get around,' Archer commented, standing over the fallen heavy.

'So do you, boy,' the other man replied evenly. 'Last time didn't end so well for you.'

'That was then,' Archer told him, 'this is now.'

'Really? You're pretty confident for a hick from the ass-end of the world.'

The man's tone was mocking and Archer felt himself getting riled. He'd always blamed this man for Bula's death, for failing to control his own men.

He took a step forward and as he did so, he saw the American's eyes flicker off-line and realised the man was smarter than he'd thought.

Archer had only half turned when the shock exploded through his body, starting at the centre of his back and flooding outwards to every fibre of his being, a 80,000 volt current blasting through him like a bolt from Hell.

He jerked and twitched and went down quickly, hitting the dirt and writhing in agony. He saw the blurry figure of the third man watching him, and heard their voices but couldn't comprehend the words through the haze that engulfed him. Someone stepped closer and kicked him in the guts, hard. It barely registered on his pain scale.

He lay there for several seconds, aware that the three men had left and he was alone again, but unable to move and struggling to gather himself. He mentally cursed his over-confidence, bitter that he'd thought himself so smart yet had fallen for such an old trick.

Eventually he hauled himself up and gingerly touched his back where the fangs of the stun gun had bitten him. He rolled his shoulders and twisted his trunk to try and shake off the pain, but even his teeth throbbed.

He checked his pockets and realised he'd been searched. It was his habit to take literally nothing when he jogged, and this time had only carried his access card for the hotel. He found it lying discarded on the dirt nearby. He wiped it off and tucked it back into his shorts pocket.

Patting himself down further, he realised the search hadn't been as thorough as it should have been. Shoved inside the waistband of his shorts was the slim wallet he'd taken from the first guy.

These two things told him something; his attackers didn't need his hotel card because they already knew where he was staying, and they were not as professional as they should be.

As he slowly limped back to his hotel, Archer wondered what exactly the point of that escapade had been. He hadn't been robbed and they hadn't taken him. Revenge? For what? An unspoken warning? Probably; but again, for what?

He didn't know and he couldn't think straight right now. But if nothing else, it had certainly woken him up properly.

19

The wide deck at the rear of the house overlooked the sweeping jungle-covered mountainside. The ocean was in the distance, blue and crisp.

A light breeze ruffled Yassar's hair as he sat at the cane table, picking at a plate of fruit – mango with a squeeze of lime, pineapple, and melon. The food was deliciously fresh and the view captivating, but Yassar could focus on nothing other than the day ahead. He had slept badly and woke with a headache. The serenity of his surroundings was little comfort for he knew the man he was with was pure evil.

Footsteps sounded on the deck behind him and his heart dropped lower.

'How's my favourite guest this morning?' Boyle's voice was loud and cheery. Yassar looked up and smiled weakly as his host plopped into the chair opposite him.

'I am very well, thank you for asking. You have a lovely spot here.'

Boyle grinned and leaned forward with an arm on the table. 'Glad to hear ye're so chipper today, lad. It's gonna be a grand day so it is, and we have a lot to get through.' He gestured towards the barely touched plate of fruit. 'Get plenty of that down ya, it's the best cure for a shitty sleep.'

'Oh, I didn't –'

Boyle's grin hadn't shifted. His eyes danced with merriment. 'Ye can't bullshit a bullshitter, Yassar. I've kissed the Blarney stone many a time and let me tell ye, I can smell yer bullshit a mile off.'

Yassar was taken aback by his manner. He wasn't used to being spoken to in such a way. He opened his mouth to speak but was cut off with a dismissive wave of the Irishman's hand and a sharp 'Tut!'

'Ye had a shitty sleep and ye're wonderin' what the fuck is gonna happen today. Well I'll tell ye. I don't like to see a man in this sort of situation, so I'll just tell ye.'

Yassar shut his mouth and waited. It seemed like he had no option anyway.

'Ye think your own crew got ye out of that hotel in Auckland? *Ehh*, wrong.' He grinned like a game show host. 'I did – even yer man Ahmed didn't know.' He shrugged. 'Shame about him, he was a good man. Yer own family have a price on yer head, ye know that?'

The Saudi arms dealer gave no acknowledgement. Boyle continued unabated.

'There's a lot of people out there who will be willing to cash that cheque, y'know.'

Yassar met his eyes and found it impossible to break away. He'd seen a crocodile once as a child – his uncle kept it in a swimming pool as a pet – and had stared at it non-stop for several minutes before realising it was a competition he would never win. He could not tell if the beast was alive or dead until it slowly lifted a paw and began to move towards him.

Staring at Boyle gave the same feeling. He was a cold blooded beast who would happily eat Yassar alive. He felt a sudden need to pee.

'Whatever it is,' Yassar managed to rasp, 'I'll double it.'

'Ha!' Boyle smiled mirthlessly. 'Ye can't.'

'I have funds...'

'But ye don't run one of the biggest arms dealerships in the world, do ye pal? Yer daddy does, and he's offerin' a cut to the man who slots his wayward son and provides his head as proof.'

Yassar's head felt it was going to explode and a tiny trickle of warm urine leaked into his underpants. There was no way on Earth he could compete with that.

Boyle sat back in the chair and tugged his ear thoughtfully.

'Me, I'm a businessman. I'm interested in makin' money. I don't particularly care who I deal with, so long as I get paid a bundle of fuckin' cold hard cash.' He glanced away, down towards the expanse of lawn below them.

Yassar followed his gaze and saw two burly Samoans hustling a slender young man from the house out onto the lawn. They each had an arm and he was powerless to resist. The boy couldn't have been more than sixteen. He was dressed in baggy shorts and a bush singlet. From where Yassar sat, the boy looked absolutely petrified.

'Ye may think I'm an unscrupulous bastard, Yassar,' Boyle continued, watching as the two men forced the boy to his knees on the grass, facing the house. 'But above all else, I have one particular passion. I hate the Brits.' His voice took on real venom now. 'I mean I hate them. If I could extinguish that God-forsaken fuckin' island from the face of the Earth, I would.'

Yassar nodded, starting to see where this was going.

'As a part of my business, I've been delivering zip-guns to the Brit gangs at knockdown prices. I make no money from it but it causes fuckin' havoc for them when the niggers and Euro-trash wannabe motherfuckers are mowin' each other down with MAC-10s.' He grinned again, happily now. 'And that brings me pleasure.'

Boyle leaned forward and put both elbows on the table.

'What would bring me even more pleasure, is helping out the angry young Islamist brothers in the UK. They have trouble getting proper weaponry and ordnance. I have a sure pipeline, but I don't have the sort of gear they need.' He tossed his chin at Yassar. 'You do.'

'I have no interest in helping the jihadists,' Yassar said weakly.

'I have no interest in those wogged-up fuckin' sand-niggers either,' Boyle retorted, 'but I do have an interest in hurting those

British monarchist bastards who raped my country. In fact I have such an interest in hurting them that I will hurt anyone who stands in my way. Take that –' he jabbed a stubby finger towards the young boy kneeling on the lawn, the two thugs standing over him – 'as an example. He's my gardener.'

Yassar glanced at the boy again. He was crying silently, tears rolling down his brown cheeks as he stared at the ground and mouthed words to himself. Praying, perhaps.

'He's been chatting online to someone, telling them all sorts of things that I trusted him to keep confidential. He believes he's been talking to a 16-year old Essex girl who's going to send him some nudie pics for his wank bank. I believe he's been talking to a member of the British intelligence services.'

'How can –'

'Oh believe me pal, I know. I know. I know how those bastards work, and I will not tolerate anyone who deals with them or breaks my trust.'

Boyle glanced down to his men and gave a tilt of the head.

The taller man drew a machete from his belt and hefted it in his hand. He took half a step back and Yassar heard a guttural sob break from the boy's lips. His eyes were screwed tight shut and he was crying hard. Yassar was mesmerised by the scene as it unfolded before him.

The machete arced down and sliced cleanly through the boy's neck, severing his head in one fell swoop. The head hit the grass with a thump, arterial blood spurted out several metres and the torso hung, momentarily suspended, before toppling forward and resting on the shoulders.

Yassar couldn't help himself. He vomited on the table.

Boyle sat back and studied him across the table. Yassar spat onto the plate and wiped his mouth with the back of his hand. He felt embarrassed. He took his time wiping his mouth and chin before spitting again and finally looking up. Boyle looked completely unaffected by the act of brutal violence they had just witnessed.

'I know for a fact that ye have a warehouse full of weaponry in

Manila,' the Irishman said calmly. 'Surface to air missiles, explosives, anti-armour, heavy machine guns, mortars, the lot.'

Yassar started to open his mouth to protest but thought better of it. He had no desire to be the next candidate down on the lawn. Boyle clocked it and gave a minute nod of agreement.

'I have the contacts to get that weaponry into the UK mainland for you. You need the cash and I want the result.'

Yassar struggled to regain some of his usual bluster. Maybe the day wasn't lost after all.

'Business is business,' he said, pursing his lips thoughtfully as if considering a marginally acceptable proposal. 'I think we can talk turkey here.'

'Make no mistake, pal,' Boyle told him flatly, 'we will do business. I want that gear and you want to live. I'll be taking that shipment off yer hands at a price that will keep me happy and you alive.'

'I have a friend in Africa who has already expressed an interest in my products,' Yassar protested. 'I cannot now renege on the deal, it would be terrible form on my part.'

'It'd be worse fuckin' form to have yer head rollin' down my fuckin' lawn, don't ya think?'

Boyle stared menacingly across the table. Two sets of footsteps sounded on the deck behind Yassar. He glanced down at the lawn and saw the two thugs had gone, along with the dismembered corpse. A dark stain remained on the grass. He knew the men were now behind him, awaiting fresh orders from their boss.

He nodded slowly and Boyle smiled.

The deal was done.

20

Archer checked his room when he got back to the hotel, but was confident it hadn't been searched.

He always took a couple of precautions when he travelled, and one of these was slipping a fragment of tissue paper between the top of the door and the frame. When he opened the door it dislodged, indicating the door had remained closed in his absence.

Archer secured the door latch and placed a chair in front of it, then stripped off and checked his body. The wound on his side had cracked and bled a little, and the stun gun had given him small twin red welts in the middle of his back.

He scowled again as he examined the new injury. He'd met the American twice now and come off second best both times. Archer was a sore loser, and he bore grudges. This guy had definitely made the list.

He drank a large glass of water as he sat brooding with an ice-pack on his back, then showered and dressed and opened the wallet he'd stolen. It was a simple plain black leather affair, with forty pounds cash, a couple of coins, a travel card dated the previous day and a debit card for one of the high street banks.

The name on the card was TJ Wheeler.

Archer laid the items out on the bed and grabbed his phone. He took a photo of the two cards and composed a quick email back to Jedi. He knew the Ops Officer wouldn't know how to get the info he wanted, but he was sure he'd know who could. He asked Jedi to try and identify the owner of the bank card, and briefly outlined the morning's incident.

That done he made his way downstairs to the dining room. There were a handful of other guests eating and Archer ignored them all, taking a copy of the Times to a corner table for two and giving his order to the waitress rather too curtly.

Moore's assessment of the full English had been accurate but Archer ate it anyway. He was ravenous and cleaned his plate, chasing it down with a glass of orange juice and two mugs of black coffee.

When Moore arrived in a cab, Archer was ready and waiting at the door, looking sharper than he felt in a charcoal Hugo Boss two-piece, a crisp white shirt, a subdued navy blue tie and polished boots. He put his black woollen coat on over the top and noted that Moore's normal attire of jeans and a bomber jacket had been replaced by a smart black suit and overcoat. Archer joined his colleague on the footpath before they walked around the corner to hail another cab.

'I met some new friends this morning,' he remarked casually, watching Moore for a reaction.

'Yeah?'

'Yeah. American. Three of them.' He paused and Moore turned away from waving at a cab, waiting for him to finish. 'Shock of my life.'

Moore frowned quizzically.

'They followed me on a run through Hyde Park, then when I bumped them I got Tasered from behind.'

Moore still didn't react, and Archer was satisfied that it was news to him.

'You sure they were Yanks?' he asked.

'100 percent sure.'

Moore frowned. 'I'd be confident they weren't from Grosvenor Square then. Or if they were, what the hell are they playing at?'

Archer watched as a cab slid in to the kerb. 'I don't know,' he replied firmly, 'but I'm gunna find out.'

The cab dropped them in a side street off Vauxhall Bridge Road, from where they walked across the bridge itself. Most of the traffic was coming towards them, into the city, but as always there were people going in every direction.

Glancing to his left, Archer could see the Security Service headquarters further along the Embankment, and he asked his companion if they would be attending the meeting.

Moore shook his head briefly. 'Unlikely. As far as I know, the sisters have no involvement in this job.' He grinned. 'But who knows?'

Ahead of them as they crossed the Thames sat the formidable headquarters of the British Security Intelligence Service. MI6. Popularly known as Legoland due to its rather block-like shape, it housed an organisation that had been attacked and scrutinised in every way possible by every foreign agency and every possible critic, and was still going strong. As far as Archer could tell from his admittedly outsider perspective, despite the odd cock-up which always fed the headlines, it was still one of the world's best spy agencies with an enviable record of success.

Security at the public entrance was rather like that of an airport, with metal detectors, an X-ray unit and closed doors off the atrium-like foyer each with card and code access. Archer followed Moore's lead, emptying his pockets for the X-ray and submitting to the scanner wand of a muscular guard who looked like an ex-Para. Their phones were surrendered and secured in a locked cabinet by the security guard.

Probably be scanned as soon as we go through, Archer figured.

Moore showed his identity card to the receptionist and a phone call was made. Archer signed in and was issued a visitor's pass to clip to his lapel.

A couple of minutes later a woman was crossing the foyer to them, smiling at Moore and extending a hand to Archer.

'Morning Rob,' she smiled, 'and you must be Craig. I'm Tracy.'
'Pleased to meet you.'

Her hand was firm and dry, and she wore a sensible grey business suit with an understated warm perfume. Her blonde hair was pulled back and her make-up was subtle. She had the leanness of a runner and the broad shoulders of a swimmer.

'Come through.'

She buzzed through a door and took them in a lift to the second floor, then into the first meeting room on the left. It was blue and plain and could have been a meeting room in any office building anywhere.

Another man entered from a door at the other end of the room with a black leather folder in his hand. He was average sized, brown haired, tidily dressed and maybe mid-forties. He carried himself confidently.

'Matthew,' he said with a pleasant smile, shaking hands with Moore first then Archer.

It was a brief, moist shake.

Tracy introduced them, and Matthew turned to Moore.

'I understand you have another matter to attend to while you're here,' he said smoothly, 'so if you don't mind...'

Moore took his cue and nodded. 'I do,' he said, opening the door behind him, 'give me a buzz when you're done, Arch.'

Archer watched him leave before they sat round the table that dominated the room. Archer noted that nobody seemed to use last names and he doubted even the first names were real. Tracy took the time to fill glasses of water from a jug on the side cabinet then deferentially took her seat beside Matthew.

'Thanks for coming in,' Matthew started, keeping his folder closed for now. 'It's good to meet you, and it's very important that we work together on this. It's a matter of great importance to both our governments. We've been aware of Yassar Al-Riyaz for some time now, keeping tabs on his movements etcetera, until he really began to move up on our radar about a year ago.'

He paused to take a sip of water. 'As you know, money's the big game now. All these terrorist organisations need it, but it's not part of the job description for the average suicide bomber. So they use these players that we've never really had dealings with before, dodgy financiers and money men from around the globe. Yassar is one of them.'

'Funny, because apparently we only became aware of him about four months ago,' Archer interjected.

Matthew nodded sagely. 'Yes,' he said, 'I know. That's something that could have been done better, and we're following up on that but it's all a bit above my pay-grade I'm afraid.'

He smiled apologetically, just one staffer sharing sympathies with his peers. Archer didn't buy it, but he was impressed with the man's political nous.

'So, you obviously know all his background already; we did manage to share that much.' Matthew chuckled at his own joke, and Tracy gave a slight smile. 'He's been in New Zealand for the last couple of months on a Visitor Visa. Interestingly, he was turned away by Australia.'

'That open borders policy just works a treat for us,' Archer remarked drily, and Matthew looked at him for a moment.

Archer got the feeling he'd spoken out of turn and felt his cheeks flush. He glanced at Tracy and saw her gaze shift as his eyes crossed her face.

Matthew continued.

'We've established links between him and a number of groups of interest to us, including the Taliban, ETA in Spain, animal activists here in the UK, rebel groups in Africa, anti-abortionists in the States...the list goes on. We have confirmed that he has handled money for all these groups, washing it through various financial institutions, making investments for them, and ultimately making them more money and giving them a clean product at the end of it all. This appears to have been on behalf of the family business.' He turned slightly towards Tracy. 'Do you want to cover our Irish friend?'

She nodded and leaned forward in her seat, taking the lead. 'A person of interest to us is a former leader in the Provisional Irish

Republican Army, Patrick Boyle. Currently living in Galway, in the Republic. He got his hands dirty growing up in Belfast during the eighties; he was part of a cell that we know for certain killed four police officers and eleven British soldiers in a series of attacks.' She looked at Archer directly to make sure he was listening. 'The four coppers were each shot dead inside their homes, in front of family members. Point blank.'

She had his attention. 'Three of the soldiers were killed in a pub in the city centre. The killer walked straight up to them and shot them point blank in the head. A fourth soldier in their group was kidnapped and held for three days. They found him on a patch of wasteland, face down. Dead. He'd been knee-capped with a drill in both knees. He was covered in burns. He had every single finger dislocated and four teeth ripped out.'

She paused unnecessarily for affect.

'It was initially thought that he'd been tortured for information, but this was discounted due to the fact that he was just a squaddie, and therefore would have very limited knowledge of use to the Provos.'

'It was practice.' Matthew took over again and Tracy hesitated, as if surprised by his interruption. When he continued, she took the hint and sat back again. 'I firmly believe that that poor kid – he was 19 – was just a practice doll for a torturer who was learning his trade. He had nothing to give them but that wasn't the point. He died in excruciating pain. The post-mortem showed the cause of death as heart failure. This was a 19-year old soldier, fighting fit, in the prime of his life.' Matthew shook his head grimly. 'His heart gave out from fear and the pain inflicted on him. We confirmed Patrick Boyle as the man responsible, and he was eventually imprisoned at the Maze. After the Good Friday Agreement, he was released.'

His eyes shifted to Archer and he looked at him mirthlessly. 'And you think your open borders cause you trouble Down Under.'

Archer held his gaze evenly, deciding he didn't like this man, not a bit. His instinct was to react, and he had to remind himself that he was operating in a new environment now. 'So what's his link to Yassar then?' he asked, breaking the moment.

'Boyle moved on from being a foot soldier to management,' replied Matthew. 'He's an educated man and has an obvious knack for financial matters. Once he was released from prison he put himself out on the market, basically operating as an investment adviser for other terrorists. You must remember, these guys have not gone away. They just operate a bit differently now, and at their core, they're basically just criminals. They make money from the whole spectrum of criminal offending and they need to launder it. That's where men like Boyle and Yassar come in.'

Matthew made a steeple of his fingers, elbows on the table. Archer noticed he still hadn't referred to whatever was in his folder.

'They have done business both together and for the same groups. They are intimately connected in a financial sense, and we know for certain that both have met with senior lieutenants to Bin Laden in recent years.'

Archer sipped his water and listened intently. He was hoping the history lesson would end soon and they'd get to the point.

'We have intelligence that these two have formed a close bond and, if it's possible for men like this, become friends. Further to that, we have intelligence that they have recently hijacked a large arms deal from Yassar's family. Yassar now has a price on his head, courtesy of his own father. Further to that, Boyle himself has a substantial amount of money stashed away somewhere. A fall back, if you like.' Matthew's eyes became shrewd now. 'We're talking circa thirty two million American.'

Archer's hand paused with the glass halfway to his lips.

'Cash,' Matthew added.

The room was silent as the information sank in.

'Wow,' Archer finally said.

'Wow is right,' Tracy smiled, and was passed the baton again with a nod from her colleague. 'It's the result of some canny investments and gambles by Boyle and Yassar.' She smiled again. 'And Her Majesty's Government would like to get their hands on it.'

Matthew smiled conspiratorially across the table. 'Of course, that is a secondary issue for us. Our Saudi friend is our main concern. And that's where you chaps come in. You see, the key is to getting our hands on either of these two men. I have no doubt that one of them will talk, given the right circumstances.' He gave a conspiratorial look. 'If you know what I mean.'

'Got a rough idea,' Archer murmured.

'Obviously British agents can't just bowl up to Boyle's little cottage in Galway and knock on the door and grab him. Those days are long gone. So when we thought our colleagues Down Under had captured Yassar and had him safely under lock and key, we were very happy campers indeed.'

Archer saw where this was going now. 'And since he escaped under our jurisdiction,' he said, 'it's our responsibility to get him back.'

Matthew smiled indulgently. 'Basically, yes. In the interests of our relationship of mutual trust and co-operation, this is rather important.'

Archer let that sit silently. The jibe was obvious and he knew the Englishman expected him to retort, but he refused to give him the satisfaction.

'I believe that Boyle is the most likely to know where Yassar is. If we get him, we can get Yassar. Once we get what we want from him, he'll be straight off to another jurisdiction.'

Archer nodded slowly. 'So I'm off to Ireland then,' he said, but Matthew shook his head.

'No,' he replied, 'you're off to Cornwall.'

21

Moore was waiting in the foyer for him when Tracy escorted Archer down.

They shook hands again and Tracy relieved him of his visitor's pass before disappearing back into the bowels of Legoland.

The two men walked back across the bridge while Archer grilled his companion about the two spooks he'd just met.

'I've met Tracy before,' Moore told him, 'she's a good girl. I've had a couple of dealings with her and she seems sound. I don't know Matthew, I know Tracy's boss is a guy called Matthew Livingstone so I'm guessing that's him.'

'What's his background?'

Archer had his hands tucked into his coat pockets and his breath was clouding in the morning chill. Jet-lag was starting to pull at him and he could do with a coffee.

'Don't know really. I heard he was previously over the river for a long time, before moving to Six.' He shrugged his big shoulders. 'Aside from that, they don't tend to chuck their CVs around, you know?'

Archer grunted. 'And the girl?'

'Tracy Spencer,' Moore replied readily, and grinned at Archer's quizzical look. 'Yeah, she reckons her Dad had a sense of humour. Ex-Army is all I really know about her, we got talking about that one day, but she didn't say too much.'

They walked in silence for a few moments. Archer debated about sharing more information with his former comrade in arms and decided against it for now. He had a lot to think about but wanted to keep it to himself. They reached the northern side of the river, and Moore pulled up short, stepping to the side of the footpath.

'I've got another meeting to go to,' he explained, casting a wary eye about him, 'you can make your own way back from here?'

Archer nodded.

'Oh, before I forget.' Moore took a small key from his pocket and passed it over. 'Your gear arrived. I'll email you the location. Locker number's on the key.'

'Ta.' Archer pocketed the key.

'I think I'll make an enquiry about these Yanks, but if I'm free later I'll give you a bell and we'll meet up for dinner,' Moore continued, and grinned. 'Watch your back mate, you're playing with the big boys now.'

He headed away down a side street towards Millbank, and Archer glanced around him, feeling suddenly self-conscious. If he was honest with himself, he'd felt out of his comfort zone with the spooks. He was getting reminded repeatedly that he was in a new world, and he wasn't sure yet that he liked it.

Tracy Spencer interested him though, he had to admit, and he looked forward to meeting her later. He waved down a cab and got dropped near the far end of Oxford Street then walked the famous shopping street back towards his hotel, taking his time and breathing in the city life around him. It was a melting pot of cultures and flavours, and in the space of a block he heard three different European languages being spoken by passing pedestrians.

Archer suddenly realised he was hungry, and checked his watch.

1115am. He found a Pret a Manger and sat in the window with a long black and a blueberry muffin, warming himself and feeling reinvigorated as the caffeine hit his bloodstream.

As he sat he began to formulate a plan in his head. Patrick Boyle had been seeing a woman in Cornwall named Ruth, who he had met when she was a teenage street worker in Belfast. She had moved to England several years ago and they had reconnected online. The relationship built to the point that he came over once a month for an overnight stay. His paranoia of the security services was still high, and he never stayed longer than twenty four hours.

His next visit was due in two days time.

The spooks knew this because prostitutes are creatures of habit. Ruth was still on the game and with that came the drugs scene. She had managed to beat a crack habit but had also become an informer for a local copper. Her information had proved credible over the years and she had eventually dropped her lover in it.

Despite having moved on from his terrorist activities, Boyle had an unhealthy fascination with guns. The timing of his monthly visits to Cornwall had been linked to the flood of firearms onto the black market, and it was believed he had access to stores previously held by the Provos. Assault rifles, sub machine guns and pistols were all readily available from dealers in the south-west.

This information had been elevated to the security services, and due to the international aspect of it MI6 – specifically Tracy – had ended up handling the informer.

The plan was to nab Boyle while he was at his mistress' house, hopefully still in possession of a shipment of weapons, giving them leverage to get at Yassar. They had no idea what weapons he may have but they knew he travelled alone, flying his private plane under the radar to a remote field. He drove to his dealers to make the transactions before heading to Ruth's place.

Archer was tasked with intercepting Boyle safely. Matthew had made it clear there would be no tactical support from either the police or military. This was strictly need-to-know. He would, however, have the services of Tracy. Once he had a basic plan in his head, Archer left the cafe and went to a nearby stationers, where he bought a map book and pens. Electronic gizmos were all well and good but Archer had a healthy appreciation for the old school.

22

Striding along the footpath, he turned into the street his hotel was on and immediately sensed trouble. A silver BMW SUV was at the kerb outside his hotel and he could see a man behind the wheel and exhaust fumes pumping from the tail pipe.

As he stepped into a doorway to watch, Archer saw two men descend the front steps of the hotel and head for the BMW. He recognised the first man as the American former sergeant, but the second man was partially obscured by him and Archer couldn't see him clearly. The sergeant moved round to the front passenger's door, and the second man opened the door behind the driver. As he did so, he cast a look over his shoulder in Archer's direction.

A cold fist gripped Archer's gut. It was the gunner who had killed Bula two years ago. The Dixie boy he'd laid out cold, and who'd been cleared of any misconduct by an inquiry.

He felt his pulse quicken as he watched the two men get in and the BMW move away from the kerb. If they were operating as a three-man team that meant the driver would be TJ Wheeler. It also meant that it had been the Dixie boy who'd Tasered him.

He'd never learned the names of the Black Star contractors

involved in the shooting, but hoped that the lead from the stolen wallet would now lead him somewhere.

As soon as the BMW turned the corner Archer made his way into the hotel, bounding up the steps into the foyer.

The receptionist behind the desk was the same Eastern European girl who'd been on duty the previous night. She was bent over something on the desk behind the counter-top, and looked up with a start when Archer strode in.

'Aahh...'

'Morning,' he said cheerily, plucking a brochure from a display on the counter-top.

It advertised guided bus tours of the city, and he held it up for her to see.

'Now tell me,' he said, 'are these tours any good? I need something to do tomorrow, but I don't want anything really touristy. What would you recommend?'

She hesitated, as if unsure whether to answer or not.

'Aahh, umm...yes, I would say they are very good, in my opinion.' She nodded vigorously, her blue eyes wide under a formidable set of false lashes.

'Lovely, thanks.' He gave her a warm smile. 'Can I order lunch here, or do I have to call room service? I've got an awful lot of work to do and I can't be bothered going out.'

'Umm, aahh, yes, if you can order here is okay.'

She produced a pad and Archer ordered a steak sandwich, fruit salad and orange juice. Giving her another smile, he went upstairs to his room.

The piece of tissue had been dislodged and was on the carpet by the door. His suitcase was on the luggage rack where he'd left it, and he noticed the zip had shifted positions slightly.

The room had clearly been searched, and he was certain that the receptionist would be on the phone right now to the Americans. While speaking to her he'd seen she had a handbag on the desk, presumably putting away the money she'd just been paid for allowing access to his room.

It was safe to assume the deal would include making a phone call once he returned.

Archer paused to think for a moment. The Americans clearly didn't want him to know they'd been there, which in turn meant they wanted to know something on the quiet. Either they had wired his room or they had been looking for something particular in his luggage. He knew there was nothing for them to find, as he had taken the stolen wallet and its contents with him.

That left the first option as the most likely.

He tossed his coat and jacket on the bed, and loosened his tie, trying to figure out what it all meant. They obviously knew who he was and who he worked for, and therefore presumably the reason for his presence in London. This made it clear they had a shared interest, but Archer couldn't determine how far that went. Were the Americans after Yassar, Boyle or both? Did they want to kill or capture either of them? Were they working for the Government or a private entity, and if so, who? Were they simply after the bounty on Yassar's head?

He decided he had more questions than answers right now, but at least he knew one thing for certain; there was a leak somewhere.

23

Archer had spent the afternoon in his room as he'd indicated to the receptionist.

The steak sandwich had been excellent and he'd had an hour's sleep to try and counter the jet-lag he'd felt creeping over him. After showering and freshening up, he dressed warmly and headed downstairs. There was a different receptionist on now, a pale young man who ignored him as he crossed the foyer.

Tracy had emailed him details of the target address in Cornwall, and he had spent some time on his notebook working out a strategy for capturing the Irishman. Moore had also been as good as his word and sent through details of where to pick up his gear that had been sent in the diplomatic pouch. He left the warm hotel and hunched his shoulders against the chill of the evening as he waited for a cab. The city was buzzing with commuter traffic and pedestrians hurrying for the Tube, and lights were on everywhere. He knew every building around him would be centrally heated and cozy and momentarily contemplated returning to his room and ordering in. Maybe he could just go and pick up his gear and be back quickly.

A black cab pulled up as he debated with himself, and he began to turn away, raising a hand in apology to the driver. He sensed a presence behind him and felt a hand grip his arm. Something hard dug into his side and Archer stiffened. A Southern drawl whispered in his ear at the same time as the cab's rear door opened.

'Be smart and get in.'

Archer realised resistance was futile right now, and moved to the door. He bent and saw the side of the driver's head. It was the Dixie boy, which meant his captor was probably the sergeant. He stepped into the back of the cab and a strong hand pushed him firmly against the far side, followed by the man's body weight hard against him. The gun barrel hadn't moved from his ribs. Archer glanced sideways and met the sergeant's steely gaze.

The cab moved off into the traffic.

'Surprised?' the sergeant asked mockingly.

'Only that you were stupid enough to kidnap me on camera,' Archer replied. 'Aside from that, no.'

The sergeant smirked. 'Kidnapped? That's pushing it a bit far, compadre. We're just a couple of old soldiers catching up. Nothin' wrong with that, is there?'

Archer gave him a disdainful look and turned his attention to the driver.

'So it'll be you I have to thank for the shocking introduction to London, then?' he asked.

The Dixie boy's eyes flicked to the rear view mirror and a grin crossed his lips.

'No thank you's are necessary, my friend.'

'Oh, I wasn't thanking you. I was just making sure I had the right person.' He paused, and the Dixie boy's eyes flicked up from the road again. 'I owe you twice now.'

The Dixie boy glanced at the sergeant now, who shook his head placatingly.

'Don't worry, pal, he's just tryin' to get inside your head.'

'No no no.' Archer shook his own head now. 'I'm not doing that, mate. I'm just making sure I have the right guy.' He met the driver's eyes again. 'Because I will kill you. That's all.' He ignored the gun in his side and leaned forward slightly, still holding the driver's gaze. 'I mean it, mate. I will kill you.'

The sergeant jerked him back against the seat and jabbed his pistol harder into Archer's side.

'Shut yer mouth, boy. Stop the trash talkin'.'

Archer ignored him and looked out the window, identifying landmarks as they drove. Heading east, he figured. Some thirty minutes later they pulled off into a side street in Leytonstone, and headed into an industrial block.

It was the sort of premises where you could rent a unit on a weekly basis, usually used by tradesmen for a specific job or by gangsters for drug dealing. There were five units in a row on each side of a driveway, and they all seemed to be closed up for the night.

The cab eased through an open door into the middle unit on the right and the door came down behind them. Lights were on inside and directly in front of the cab was an office with a set of stairs going up the side wall to a storage area above the office. Standing on the stairs was the guy Archer had bumped in the park, cradling a suppressed Beretta M12 chopper in his hands, watching the new arrivals.

TJ Wheeler.

Archer glanced quickly around, getting his bearings and scoping any possible weapons or escape routes. Stacked against the left wall were bags of garden fertiliser, enough to fill a Transit van. Directly ahead were six fuel drums.

The sergeant caught his eye and smirked as if reading his mind.

The driver got out and opened the door, and Archer alighted. He paused and looked coldly at the Dixie boy across the top of the door. The younger man flinched but held his gaze.

'Your days are numbered, kid,' Archer told him softly.

'Yer in no position to be making threats right now, boy,' the sergeant told him, and pushed him against the side of the cab.

While the others covered him the Dixie boy searched Archer roughly, emptying his pockets and efficiently checking every possible hiding place without stripping him. As the young man's hand explored his crotch, Archer let out a snort.

'I knew you'd linger.'

The Dixie boy let go immediately and slammed him into the side of the car. Archer's face bounced off the pillar and he took a knee in the side of his thigh, causing his leg to buckle.

The sergeant stepped in and pulled the Dixie boy away. 'Ease up, don't damage the goods.' He grabbed Archer by the arm and hustled him to the office, shoving him through the door. 'Get in there.'

Archer stumbled into the unfurnished office and was still turning to face them when a rabbit punch caught him behind the ear, sending him crashing against the back wall. The room was only about four metres square and faced with a glass door and windows either side of it. The two mercenaries faced him from the door. There was not a single item in the room that he could use as a weapon. The carpet was worn completely flat and the walls were bare.

'Make it easy on yerself, boy,' the sergeant told him calmly, holding his compact pistol loosely at his side. It looked like a stainless Walther, a common back up weapon amongst operators. 'Lose the tough guy act and start listenin'.'

'Do we have to talk? Can't we just go for dinner and a movie?'

The sergeant ignored him and stepped aside to let the Dixie boy join them. He had a large pistol in his hand and was loading a feathered dart into the breech.

Archer gave a wry smile. 'What is this, amateur hour?' He gestured towards the vehicle bay. 'A load of fertiliser and fuel, I'm lying here drugged to the eyeballs, an anonymous phone call to the cops...' He shook his head.

'That's the basic idea, yeah.'

'You guys don't get any smarter, do you?'

'Shut yer mouth, dickwad,' the Dixie boy snarled, cocking the dart gun.

'Witty,' Archer commented, 'clearly you're the brains of this fuckin' shambles. I bet your mother-sister is really proud.'

'Enough talkin',' the sergeant interrupted. 'Time for you to start listenin'. This ain't a joke.' He leaned against the doorframe and waggled the pistol at him. 'We tried playin' nice but it didn't get through.'

'Oh, is that what you call it?' Archer nodded his understanding. 'Sorry, my fault. Here was me thinking it was just another cheap shot from behind.'

The Dixie boy bristled and looked to the sergeant. The older man was unruffled.

'You needed to butt out and fuck off back to the ass end of the world where y'all come from. If you can't take the hint, well...maybe we need to be more direct.'

'A little bit obvious, don't you think?'

'In this world?' The sergeant let out a laugh. 'Everybody jumpin' at their own shadow? Raghead terrorists behind every pot plant? The Brits'll be all over you like a fat chick at a buffet, boy.'

'Good one, Carl,' the Dixie boy chuckled, and the sergeant shot him a scowl.

'So Carl, TJ and sorry, I didn't catch your name?'

'Enough.' The sergeant waved for the Dixie boy to get on with it. 'Stop jawin' and do it.'

Archer gave the Dixie boy a mocking smile. 'I bet you love jawin' him, don't you?' he sneered.

The Dixie boy immediately threw a questioning look to his boss, and Archer knew he'd pegged them right; the younger man was a hot head but unsure if his boss would back him. In the split second the two mercenaries looked at each other, Archer seized his opportunity. He sprang forward and lashed out with a frontal kick at the sergeant's gun, connecting hard enough to make the other man involuntarily trigger a shot that was deafening in the small room.

The Dixie boy grabbed at him and Archer spun, seizing the outstretched hand and yanking him forward, pinning Carl in the corner. He snatched at the hand holding the dart gun and twisted savagely, bringing a yelp of pain. The Dixie boy tried for a head butt. Archer took it on the shoulder and smashed his elbow into his opponent's face.

Carl was pushing them both away and bringing the pistol around when Archer twisted the Dixie boy's wrist harder. A bone snapped audibly and the Dixie boy yelped again. Archer forced his own finger into the trigger guard and squeezed, pumping the dart into Carl's side.

He slammed a knee up into the Dixie boy's groin and shoved him away, ducked and caught Carl's swinging arm, locked it straight and drove the heel of his palm up and through the joint, obliterating the elbow.

The sergeant's face went white and he shrieked in pain, popping off a second shot which shattered the glass in the door. Archer slammed his forehead into Carl's nose and flattened it in a spray of blood. He dropped him and ripped the pistol from his hand.

As the man fell TJ came into view, the Beretta up and flashing a short burst through the shattered door, rounds buzzing past Archer's shoulder. He dived to the side and snapped off a double tap, realising he was trapped in the room with the only exit covered by a chopper.

TJ risked a glance around the window frame and Archer fired again, blowing out the glass. Glancing down, he saw the Dixie boy struggling to pull a weapon from where he lay on the floor. Knowing he had at best only three rounds left, Archer threw himself forward in a slide, crashing both feet into the boy's torso and knocking the gun away. He drove his heel into the boy's face and as he pulled back for another go, saw TJ's head come into view above him in the shattered window frame.

The merc was scanning the room with the SMG's suppressor following his eyes, not realising Archer had moved. He never had a chance. Archer squeezed off a double tap that took him in the temple and spread his brains across the wall. The slide locked open and Archer rolled to his feet, checking for threats.

TJ was in a heap on the floor by the cab, blood running freely from his head. Carl was unconscious but moaning, his shattered arm lying grotesquely at his side. The Dixie boy was twitching and groaning, the crotch of his pants soaked wet.

Archer tossed the empty pistol aside and snatched up the Dixie boy's gun. It was a stainless Walther PPK/S like his partner's. He kicked the Dixie boy in the ribs, getting his attention.

'You've got about a minute to fill me in,' he said coldly, pointing the gun at the boy's face.

The boy groaned in pain and shifted his gaze.

'Who are you working for? The Saudis? IRA?'

The boy groaned again and Archer kicked him harder.

'Who's calling the shots, kid? The Agency?'

The boy struggled to focus through his pain, and bared his bloodied teeth.

'Fuck you,' he croaked, blood smeared on his teeth as he grimaced, 'and fuck that nigger boy too.'

Archer ground his foot down on the boy's kneecap, producing a squeal. The Dixie boy grabbed for his knee with his uninjured hand, leaving his broken wrist exposed. Archer's foot was on it in a second, first applying light pressure. The merc squealed again and Archer pressed harder.

'Talk or I'll fuck you up completely,' he said softly. 'You'll be wiping your arse and jerking off with one hand till the day you die.'

'Fuck man.' The Dixie boy flailed weakly at Archer's leg. 'C'mon man, you're fuckin' cripplin' me.'

'Not yet, but I will. Who're you working for? Who organised all this?' Archer knew he wouldn't have much time.

The Dixie boy tossed his head at the still form of his boss. 'He knows man, ask him.'

'He's out cold; I'm asking you.'

'I dunno man, he's the boss. I'm just a grunt, man.' His eyes were wet and pleading as Archer trod harder on his shattered wrist, grinding the broken bone under his sole. The merc's face was a sickly shade of pale green. 'C'mon man! I need a fuckin' doctor, I'm no use to you.'

Archer's head twitched slightly in acceptance. 'That's true.'

He calmly shot him between the eyes. The body convulsed then lay twitching. The right leg drummed a brief solo on the floor.

24

Archer checked the sergeant's pulse; out for the count.

He quickly searched all three bodies, retrieving cell phones and wallets, before wiping down both pistols. He carefully placed them back in their respective owner's hands.

Moving to the front of the unit he cracked open the pedestrian door beside the main roller and listened. Sirens sounded some way off, but closer in he could hear the roar of car engines being pushed hard, less than a click away.

He swung on the chain to raise the roller door, gathered his own belongings and the items he'd seized from his captors, and fired up the cab.

Within seconds of reaching the main road a Police car flew by him towards the industrial units, another couple only seconds behind it. He spotted a chopper approaching as well and maintained a steady speed as he made his way back towards the city. He tried calling Moore several times on the way, but every time it went straight to voicemail. He left a short message wanting a call back.

Tucking his phone away, he debated passing the details of the Yank team back to Jedi. Instinct told him to hold back just yet, at least until he'd spoken to Moore and knew the lay of the land.

For now, he was on his own. He dumped the cab in a Tower Hamlets side road and walked away, covering a mile before hailing a cab to Euston station.

Two further cab rides took Archer back to Marble Arch, where he spent another half hour scouring the block for a back up team. Finding none, and with his heart rate back under control, he ducked into the closest pub and ordered a large Scotch on the rocks.

The barmaid was a busty brunette with French nails and a cheeky grin. Her name tag said Becky. She let her fingers linger on his as she gave him his change. Archer knocked half the drink back and let the peaty warmth slide down his throat into his gut.

So much for a quiet dinner out, he reflected, realising he was still hungry. Instead of a hot pot and a pint he'd killed two men, maimed a third and probably started an international incident.

He caught the barmaid's eye and asked for a bar menu.

'Kitchen's closed sorry love,' she said, leaning forward on the bar and giving him a full view of her plentiful cleavage. 'Closed at eight.' She glanced over her shoulder to check for the manager and gave him the cheeky grin. 'I could probably whip something up for you though, if you give me twenty minutes.'

Archer nodded. 'Sweet, I'll wait.' He drained his tumbler and slid another twenty across the bar. He let his eyes linger on her cleavage, knowing she was watching him. 'I'll need another drink to cool down.'

The tops of her breasts shook as she gave a throaty chuckle. 'No problem.'

He took the fresh drink to a corner booth and nursed it while he waited, surveying the punters around him. Nobody gave off any warning signals, and no matter how often he checked his phone, Moore didn't call back.

Becky brought him a plate of butter chicken on microwaved rice with a garlic naan, and was hailed back to the bar by a punter before she could speak. She rolled her eyes, gave Archer a wink and sauntered back to the bar, tossing him a look over her shoulder as she did so. She was not thin but had a roll to her hips that he liked.

The sauce was from a jar and the food had been reheated, but he ate hungrily, mopping his plate with the naan and sitting back with a satisfied sigh. Becky returned and cleared the plate, bending over close enough for him to smell her dusky perfume. There was no mistaking her intentions.

'I knock off in an hour,' she told him, a glint in her eye and her voice soft in his ear. 'You fancy sticking around for a bit?'

Archer smiled and nodded. 'Maybe I should.' He gave her his empty tumbler. 'Better make that a pint then.'

She disappeared and he rubbed his face. The alcohol and the downer after the adrenaline wore off were making him tired. He needed a pick-me-up. He was planning his night with the busty Becky when his phone buzzed. The caller ID showed Private Number.

Expecting Moore, he was surprised to hear a female's voice when he answered.

'Craig, it's Tracy Spencer. We've got a goer, he's coming early. I'll pick you up in forty five minutes.'

He was silent as he absorbed the news.

'Are you there?'

'Yeah...yeah, I'm here. See you in forty five.'

He disconnected and moved for the door, focussed now on the job at hand. Becky intercepted him before he got there, looking confused.

'Oi, what you playin' at? I thought...'

'I'm sorry, I've gotta go.' He smiled what he hoped was apologetically. 'Work called me in, sorry.'

'Whatev's.' She tossed her hair dismissively and turned away. 'Your loss, love.'

Archer stepped after her and whispered in her ear. 'Don't you worry, love, I'll see you again.' Her musk filled his nostrils and she pressed back against him.

He squeezed her arm and went for the door.

25

Tracy slid to the kerb in a non-descript gunmetal grey Saab 9000 Turbo exactly forty five minutes later.

Archer slung his bags in the boot beside hers and took the passenger seat. A pair of service station coffees sat in the cup holder.

'I figured I should make it worth your while to get pulled away at this time of night,' she said apologetically as she accelerated away. 'You look like a long black kind of a bloke.'

'Any coffee's good coffee,' he replied, buckling himself in.

She was heavy on both pedals and used the automatic gears as if they were manual. He steadied himself before taking his coffee. It was hot and strong and the aroma alone was enough to give him a boost.

Tracy smelled of a popular perfume he couldn't quite place, warm spicy vanilla, and was dressed for work in jeans and a thermal top. She turned the radio down as they headed for the M25.

'Boyle's coming over tomorrow night. I had a call from the informant, he's due at hers by dawn – he's promised her a dawn breaker to remember.'

Archer nodded and savoured a mouthful of coffee. It always

tasted better when you were drinking with a girl, he reflected. 'Is this normal for him to come at the last minute?' he asked.

Tracy's strong hands worked the gears and wheel as she took the motorway on ramp at speed. Archer slipped his cup back into the holder for safe keeping. Tracy noticed and grinned.

'Not scared are you? I thought all you triggermen were tough as nails?'

Triggermen? If only you knew.

He grunted. 'The only things that scare me are women drivers and the tax man.'

Tracy hit the fast lane and held a steady ninety, reaching for her own cup. Archer passed it to her, pausing to sniff the mouth of it first.

'Cappuccino? No...long black with sweetener.'

'Well done.' She sipped it appreciatively. 'And yes, it's not uncommon for him to come over at short notice. He always contacts her though, to make sure she doesn't have any other commitments first.' She snorted. 'He's considerate like that.'

'What a catch. By commitments I take it you mean clients?'

'Mostly. She also plays bridge in a local club though, and visits her gran most days.'

'And enjoys moonlit walks on the beach and Tom Hanks romcoms,' Archer replied.

Tracy shot him a sideways glance. 'Wow, heavy on the sarcasm there, Kiwi.'

'Kiwi? Really?' He smiled, enjoying her sassiness.

'I'm working with that for now. Colonial's a bit of a mouthful, Antipodean's even worse.' She frowned as she overtook a lorry with one hand on the wheel. 'And what's an Antipodean, anyway? Does anyone actually ever go to the Antipodes?'

'Not since early last century. Or maybe around the forties, when we had to save the Poms' sorry arse. Again.'

Tracy grinned at his needling. 'Pom? Is that the best you can do? It doesn't even mean anything anyway.'

'Prisoner of Mother England,' he said. 'Means you're all still tied to the monarchy with floral apron strings.'

They fell into a comfortable silence for a time, and Archer let his mind wander back to the events earlier in the evening. It still puzzled him what the motive was for the American mercenaries. If they were working for the Yank government, the CIA or DIA or whoever, they could have just leaned on his own bosses or the Brits and taken over the mission lock stock and barrel.

No, the back door tactics didn't fly with that scenario. In the War on Terror, the US got their own way, no issues there. Everything he knew to date indicated something different entirely. There was a different puppet master pulling the strings on this one, somebody unofficial but with significant clout; PMCs did not come cheap.

Archer turned his mind to the men themselves, the men he'd killed without batting an eyelid. He felt no remorse at all, not a drop. They were cold blooded killers themselves; they knew the score. If it wasn't them it would've been him. Two lay dead and the leader, Carl, faced a lot of difficult questions from the police followed by a life with a crippled arm.

Archer took a certain malevolent satisfaction from knowing he'd taken them out of the game, particularly the Dixie boy who'd murdered Bula so long ago. He'd gone through all three cell phones, and found they were clearly all burn phones; cheap pre-pays used for a job then discarded. He'd recorded all the numbers out of them – no saved contacts – and emailed them to himself to check later.

He wondered again why Moore hadn't got back to him, and checked his phone. No missed calls, no messages. He tucked it away and watched Tracy in his peripheral vision. She drove with confidence and seemed more at ease now, even excited, without Matthew Livingstone looking over her shoulder.

He liked her enthusiasm and so far she seemed competent. Time would tell. He had to admit he found her attractive in the way women in the armed forces often were – for some reason guns and girls could be an intoxicating blend. But as with any mission Archer felt nervous anticipation about the task ahead of them, and this was increased by the unknown factor of Tracy.

He was used to working with highly trained men, combat

veterans who had been proven under fire. He'd never gone into the field with a woman in tow, let alone a female spy. It made him feel uneasy. After a time they stopped at a service centre for more coffee and sandwiches and a rest stop for Tracy.

While he waited for the coffee order he tried calling Moore again, but still got his voicemail. He left another message and scoffed his sandwiches while he waited. He bought some bottled water, chocolate bars and energy drinks as well, and took the lot back to the car. He quickly checked the boot to make sure nothing had been disturbed – he'd just had time after Tracy's call to go and fetch his bag from the locker where Moore had stashed it, and had beaten Tracy back to the hotel by barely a minute. He had no intention of giving her a heads up on his weaponry just yet.

When Tracy returned he cheerily offered to drive so she could eat.

He had no doubt she'd seen through the flimsy excuse but she handed the keys over anyway and eased back the passenger seat. She took a sip of her cup and gave him a surprised look.

'Hot chocolate? What am I, eighty? Is this Horlicks?'

Archer smiled. 'Too much caffeine and you won't sleep. I need you rested when we get there. We won't get a second chance at this.'

Tracy didn't reply, burrowing instead into the plastic bag of food. She came out with a Yorkie bar and held it up questioningly. 'Just think of yourself then, won't you?'

Archer looked confused.

'Not for girls,' she explained. 'I can't have that, I might hurt myself. You obviously haven't seen the ad.'

She half grinned then and Archer relaxed, feeling the last of the ice break. He eased back onto the highway and accelerated hard, wanting to make time so they were in place well before Boyle arrived. Tracy was soon asleep and Archer settled into the drive, enjoying the almost empty rural highways and the power of the Saab.

He mentally ran through risks and potential tactics as he drove, but it was difficult to assess without knowing the real details of the mission. The glaringly obvious risk to him right now was his partner, who was stirring from sleep. She cranked the seat up and rubbed her eyes.

As if reading his thoughts, Tracy glanced sideways and caught him looking away.

'Worried?' she asked.

'Not worried,' he replied. 'Just working it through in my head.'

'It'll be alright,' she told him with the hint of a smile. 'I am trained, you know.'

Archer grunted and raised a quizzical eyebrow.

'I joined the Army from school,' she told him, and reaching for her coffee as he dropped into the middle lane. 'My Dad was a soldier, did all the usuals for his generation – the Falklands, Northern Ireland, the first Gulf War. I grew up on Army bases in the UK and Germany. I couldn't wait to join when I was a kid, listening to his stories and meeting his mates. I spent a lot of time hanging round the bases soaking it all in.' She laughed. 'I liked playing war more than my brother. He went and became a doctor and I spent ten years as an MP.'

Archer said nothing, draining his coffee instead and staring out the window at the darkness beyond the highway.

'So where exactly are we going?' he asked finally. 'Cornwall's a big place.'

Tracy was silent for a moment, as if weighing up her answer. 'We're going to Hampshire first,' she replied, 'the Firm's got a little place on the coast.'

26

The description of "a little place on the coast" was misleading at best.

Fort Monckton was an ancient fort perched on a cliff top, overlooking Stokes Bay in Gosport. They swapped drivers again before they got there and Tracy seemed to follow her nose in the darkness.

A civilian security guard met them at a barrier arm on the approach road and Tracy buzzed her window down, letting in a blast of cold air. After checking her credentials he stepped back from the car and spoke into a walkie talkie, presumably calling his ops base. Archer and Tracy silently watched him as he frowned and listened before coming back to the window.

'Sorry madam,' he said in a broad West Country burr, 'but alternative arrangements have been made for you.'

Tracy frowned. 'Are you sure? I wasn't aware…we're supposed to be meeting here.'

'Sorry madam,' he repeated, and gave Archer a furtive glance. 'I've been told to redirect you to the Holiday Inn at Portsmouth. Reservations have been made…'

He glanced at Archer again and looked uncomfortable. Archer

scowled and shook his head in frustration. 'Was that from Mr Livingstone?' he said pointedly, and the guard shrugged non-committally.

''Fraid I don't know, sir. I just gets me orders, like.'

'So much for trust and co-operation,' Archer muttered darkly.

Tracy said nothing, just buzzed the window up and did a quick J-turn before heading back the way they'd come. Archer expected her to stop and call Livingstone and when she continued driving instead, he broke the tense silence.

'Is this normal?' he asked. She stayed focussed on the road ahead as she nosed towards the Holiday Inn.

'Don't worry about it,' she replied finally, 'it's no big deal.'

Archer snorted. 'It kind of is, really, when you get invited into the club but aren't allowed into the clubhouse.'

'It's not like that. He's not trying to exclude you.'

'Course he is, he's an arrogant snob. Doesn't anyone ever question Golden Boy Livingstone, or is that just not the done thing in your outfit?'

Tracy threw him an angry glance. 'Nobody needs to question him, because he's bloody good at his job. He's the go-to guy for us, and this is a huge opportunity for me to be able to work with him. You should look at it the same way – you might actually learn something.'

'Like how to win friends and influence people? No thanks.'

'What Mathew doesn't know about the intelligence world isn't worth knowing,' Tracy snapped. 'He's done everything and re-wrote the book, so don't write him off just because he doesn't want to be your bosom buddy. That's his way. He has the ear of some very high level people; he's on first name terms with the Foreign Secretary, for God's sake.'

Neither of them spoke until they arrived at the hotel and roused the night porter. Tracy checked them in while Archer got the bags. The hotel was silent aside from the background chatter of a Bollywood movie on the porter's portable DVD player.

Tracy slid Archer's key along the Reception desk to him and

grabbed her bag. 'See you in the morning,' she tossed over her shoulder before turning and walking away.

Archer and the porter looked at each other. The porter smirked. Archer shrugged and scooped up the key, following the stiff back in front of him, noticing again the tautness of her buttocks as she climbed the stairs.

She didn't look back as she swiped into her room and shut the door. Archer mentally dismissed her and entered the room across the hall. He tossed his bag onto the luggage shelf and flicked on the TV. The room was basic and formulaic.

No expense spared; thanks Matt.

Except somebody like him would never be called Matt; that just wouldn't be proper. Surprising he didn't have a double-barrelled last name. Archer put the jug on and booted up his laptop. He opened up his email to himself with the details taken from phones of the American crew. It was only a handful of numbers that had been called, and he quickly realised they had mostly called each other. The texts between themselves were brief and meaningless.

He forwarded the email to Jedi with a short explanation of what had happened then shut the laptop down and flopped onto the bed. No matter how he tried to push it aside, Tracy's mood bugged him. Something about her had got under his skin and it bothered him that she was annoyed.

Twice he got up and went to the door before cursing himself for acting like a fawning schoolboy. Finally he caved and opened the door, striding across the hall and raising his hand to knock. He paused and decided again he was being foolish, and was turning to retreat when he heard movement and the door opened.

Tracy stood and arched an eyebrow at him. She wore striped pyjama pants and a plain white singlet that did nothing to hide her protruding nipples. Archer glanced down automatically then flushed as he looked up and caught her eye.

'Is this a social visit or what?' she asked pointedly.

'Ahh...I just...what time are we heading off in the morning? I just...I'll go for a run, that's all.' It sounded lame and he knew it.

'I'll meet you for breakfast at seven,' she said abruptly, and made to shut the door.

He stayed where he was, and she paused.

'Was there something else?'

Archer shook his head and turned away, hearing the door close behind him. Once inside his own room he mentally gave himself a swift uppercut before bed.

He'd barely closed his eyes when his cell phone rang. It was Jedi.

'Have you gone off the fucking reservation?' the former RSM demanded.

Archer sat up and fumbled for the bedside light, trying to gather himself. He'd been bollocked once before by Jedi – WO1's were allowed to do that to officers – and he had the immediate impression this was about to be number two.

'No, but I think they did.'

'They're not on the books. Moore checked.' Jedi's tone was terse and edgy. 'Our friends don't tend to bullshit us about that sort of thing, not when two of their countrymen are dead and a third is found with the murder weapon and saying nothing.'

'I tried to get hold of Rob…'

'He was meeting a high level source. And yes, this line is secure, by the way.'

Archer was tired and getting sick of being jerked about. 'I can't change the facts, Jedi. They called the play and I responded appropriately. Would you rather it was a Kiwi found with a shed load of explosives and some bullshit story? It'd be me down at Paddington Green getting grilled right now, and probably all over the papers tomorrow.'

Jedi was silent and Archer could almost feel the heat down the phone line. He decided to push his case home.

'Instead of getting into me, why not ask the Yanks why they don't have their dogs on a fuckin' leash? It's all very well saying they're not on the books, but they were in London for a reason and it crosses into this job. They wanted me out of the way, so if their Government wasn't calling the shots then who was? It was somebody in the know.'

'That's a pretty short list,' Jedi responded. Some of the sting had gone out of his voice and Archer knew he was hitting the mark.

'So it shouldn't be too hard to figure out then. Besides, the Agency or whoever already bailed those pricks out once, so why not again? They're obviously important assets.'

'I made those checks. I take it you realise you've met these guys before.' It wasn't a question but Archer nodded to himself anyway.

'I do,' he said curtly.

'Carl Miller, Terence Wheeler, Thad Sychak. Miller and Wheeler are ex-Airborne, served with distinction but were busted for stealing weapons and selling them on the black market. Went private after that. Sychak did about a year as a grunt and was dishonourably discharged, apparently for general shit kicker behaviour. Assaulted a black officer and threatened to lynch him.'

Archer snorted but wasn't surprised. 'And this is who the Yanks get to do their dirty work?'

Jedi was silent again and Archer waited. He had nothing else to say and was ready to fight his corner. The silence last almost a minute and Archer wondered if he'd lost the connection, until Jedi came back on.

'We'll look into it further,' he said, 'and I'll come back to you. In the meantime, watch your back.'

27

The next morning Archer hit the floor at 5:30am and threw on his running gear.

After a warm up he ran hard for twenty minutes through Southsea, before returning to the hotel sweaty and breathing hard.

He rinsed off in his room and changed into togs, detecting no movement from Tracy's room as he padded his way silently down to the leisure centre. The pool was empty and still and he barely made a ripple as he dived smoothly in. He didn't count his lengths but just kept going, strong and rhythmic, until the G-Shock told him it had been half an hour.

He touched the wall for the last time and hauled himself up onto the side, his chest heaving as he wiped his face clear and sucked in air. He could hear the clank of weights through in the gym, and wondered who else would be up this early. Grabbing his towel, he quickly rubbed himself down before circling the pool to the gym door. He peered through the head height window.

The only occupant was Tracy, using a machine for lat pulldowns. From where he stood he could see the muscles working in her shoulders and back as she smoothly pulled the bar down behind her head, paused, let it raise slightly and paused once more before slowly releasing it up again. She wore a black Lycra crop top and shorts that revealed plenty of firm, toned flesh. She was totally focussed on her set and he stepped away before he got caught staring again.

Archer shook his head at himself as he headed back to his room. 'Jesus,' he muttered, 'get a fuckin' grip.'

Tracy didn't show at the restaurant until he was nearly finished his second bowl of muesli and fruit. She threw him a quick smile as she helped herself to coffee and porridge, and once she sat down he felt a change in the dynamics from the previous night.

She told him in a whisper that they were meeting Matthew at 8:00am and would deploy from there. Her skin glowed with the recent exercise, and as she raised her spoon to eat he noticed she had a faint white scar between the middle two knuckles on her right hand.

She saw him looking. 'A misplaced punch,' she explained. 'Top left incisor of a drunk squaddie who tried his luck one night.'

'Ouch.'

'More ouch for him when my eighteen stone partner lifted him off the ground and threw him across the barroom.' She smiled. 'It's an effective way of scaring the crap out of a bunch of raw recruits.'

Archer drained his cup and set it down. There was nobody sitting near them and it seemed like an appropriate time. 'So, ten years as a "Red Cap." Must've been a pretty tough life for a young chick.'

'It had its moments,' she acknowledged, finishing her porridge and pushing the bowl aside. 'There're no shortage of stupid young blokes who need to be pulled into line, that's for sure.'

'See any combat though?' Archer replied, with more of an edge than he'd intended. 'Ever killed anyone? Been under fire?'

Tracy's eyes flashed angrily and she paused before replying.

'I did two tours in Iraq,' she said coldly, 'I came under fire, I returned fire, I had mates killed and I made it out alive. So don't talk down to me like some school kid, you arrogant fuckin' prick.'

Archer raised his hands in surrender. 'Alright, alright, calm down. I didn't know, okay? You never said.'

'Well, you never asked either, did you?' Her tone was still angry. 'What else do you want to know?'

'Have you killed before?' He held her gaze, and picked up the tiny flicker of a tell. 'That's a no, then.'

She opened her mouth to retort and he cut her off.

'It's okay, I just needed to know.'

She visibly relented slightly, without properly backing up.

'It's not such a big deal, it may not even get to that. Hopefully, anyway.'

Tracy watched him critically. 'You're obviously new to this game yourself, so I'm guessing you're probably fresh out the black pyjama outfit.' Her eyes crinkled as he inclined his head to acknowledge the truth of her assessment. 'It's written all over you, you can almost still smell the cordite leaking out your pores.'

Archer shifted uncomfortably under her gaze. He wasn't used to being under the spotlight like this.

'Obviously an officer,' she continued, 'because you have that arrogance about you.'

'Which makes you an NCO,' he replied evenly, 'I'm guessing probably still a Corporal after ten years, meaning you were frustrated at being overlooked for promotion for less-competent blokes, and ultimately left before your time.'

It was her turn to give the slightest of nods, accompanied by a twitch of a smile. 'It's still a boy's club, and always will be.'

They both went silent as they absorbed the information they'd just gleaned from each other.

'I'm picking you as a committed bachelor,' Tracy added. 'No sign of a ring, no tan line where you've removed it – and you obviously fancy yourself as something of a ladies' man anyway.'

Archer cocked his eyebrow again. 'Glad you noticed. For a single mum, you work in a dangerous game.'

Tracy looked surprised. 'Really? A single mum?'

He nodded. 'I'm not claiming to be a detective like you, but I know things about people.' He ran an eye over her. 'I can see it in you.' He thought, but kept it to himself, *and you probably bat for the other team as well.*

'My boy is nine,' she told him, and added nothing further.

Archer took the hint and didn't mind. He didn't know a lot about kids and had little interest in discussing them. 'Right, so that's that then,' he smiled. 'Glad we cleared the air. Let's go meet with your illustrious leader.'

28

The meeting place turned out to be an annex building at the Royal Navy base in Portsmouth. They were ushered inside by a couple of goons in suits, who closed the meeting room doors behind them and took up sentry outside.

Matthew Livingstone sat at a conference table, working on a laptop connected to a projector. A young female in a business suit sat off to one side with a tablet on her knee. She nodded but said nothing. Livingstone gave a cursory greeting as they sat down, before jumping straight into a briefing.

The young female dimmed the lights and an area map showed on the wall. Using a laser pointer, Livingstone highlighted areas of interest. Despite disliking the man Archer had to admit he gave a good briefing, which was largely a rehash of what Tracy had told him the night before, augmented with a few finer details.

'Now,' Livingstone finally said, hitting a button to change the map view. It shifted to an aerial shot of farmland with a road running along near the bottom, and what looked like a rough farm track meandering through it. 'Let's talk tactics.'

Archer sat up and paid attention. This was the nitty-gritty of it.

'This paddock here is where we know Boyle lands his plane. It is basically level and makes an ideal makeshift landing strip. The track here' – he indicated with the laser pointer – 'leads from the strip to the road, and from there he makes his way to St Ives. He stashes his car somewhere around here' – another indication with the laser pointer, this time to the wooded area immediately beside the paddock – 'and returns it later.'

'How do we know this?' Archer inquired and Livingstone paused. He seemed to be considering his answer.

'Aerial reconnaissance has revealed the track to be well used, and has also located a car stashed in the woods there. An old Peugeot, actually.'

He turned back towards the image on the wall to continue.

'How do we know it's his car?' Archer persisted.

Livingstone looked at him again, his lips pursing. 'Our CHIS has told us that's what he drives.'

Archer knew what he was referring to but feigned confusion. 'CHIS?'

'Covert Human Intelligence Source,' Tracy explained. 'An informer.'

Archer nodded his understanding and Livingstone gave him an enquiring look.

'Anything else Mr Archer, or can I continue?'

Archer smiled irritatingly. 'Please do.'

'So, tactics. The plan is to capture Boyle as soon as he hits the ground. We don't want him going mobile, either in the aircraft or in the car. If that happens we have a real issue on our hands. We need to be in quickly, overpowering him and getting him away before he knows which way is up.'

Archer listened silently.

'This will be a simple two-person snatch and grab. You'll locate the vehicle and disable it, eliminating that avenue of escape. You'll lay-up between his landing area and the vehicle. Once he's out and away from the aircraft you'll take him out using distraction devices, and if necessary, bean bag rounds.'

Archer listened, his face impassive.

'You'll secure him straight into a vehicle and bring him to an RV where he will be taken off your hands quick smart.' Livingstone glanced from Archer to Tracy and back again. 'Any questions so far?'

'No,' Tracy replied.

'Only one, really,' Archer commented.

Livingstone looked at him impatiently. 'Yes? Well?'

'Who was the halfwit who thought up that plan?'

Tracy groaned audibly and tried to cover it with a cough. Livingstone flushed angrily.

'That plan is ideal for this situation,' he snapped, jabbing the table top with his finger. 'It keeps it contained from the public, off the roads and totally within our control. This man is a very dangerous terrorist, he is always armed and he will not hesitate to shoot.'

Archer let him finish his rant and waited. 'I counted three separate farmhouses within a k or so of that landing strip,' he said. 'Presumably all are occupied.'

'Yes, well, what of it?'

'That's three sets of potential hostages if he gets loose and goes on the run. It's three sets of potential witnesses to a shootout when we slot him and end up in court on murder charges. It's three sets of star witnesses selling their story to the tabloids if anything goes wrong.' He paused to let that sink in. 'See what I mean?'

Livingstone snorted. 'Well if you do it properly, none of that will happen, will it?'

'We can do everything right and try to minimise the risk, but the potential is always there. If it can go wrong, it will.' He went for the buddy buy-in. 'You've been around long enough; you know that.'

Livingstone grunted begrudgingly now. Tracy stayed silent, watching the two men verbally parry and thrust.

'So what do you suggest?' the senior spy finally said.

'Leave it with me,' Archer told him. 'I'll get back to you.'

29

Boyle settled behind the wheel of the Peugeot and cranked up the heater.

His fingertips were numb and he had drained the flask of coffee already. Not to mind; Ruth always had a hot breakfast waiting when he got there.

Soon enough, he thought, bumping down the farm track to the road. But no time to think about that just yet. This was the most dangerous time, early hours of the morning when the body was screaming out for sleep. Had to have your wits about you.

He shifted the Browning under his right thigh and checked his mirrors again before easing out onto the road. Six miles to St Ives.

Tracy saw the dirty white Peugeot approaching through the scope on the Heckler and Koch G3/HK79 combo. She pressed the talk button taped to her thumb.

'Twenty seconds.'

'Roger.' Archer's voice came through the bud in her ear and she could hear the sound of the engine in the background.

She was positioned flat on a bank with a ghillie over her and a clear line of sight down the route being taken by Boyle. In fifteen seconds he would reach the T-intersection below her position and because of the narrow winding roads, he would have to come to almost a complete stop before turning right and continuing on towards St Ives.

Archer appeared from Tracy's left, rounding a bend in a hired VW Kombi. It was painted with large multi coloured flowers and peace signs. Streamers flapped from the aerial and the rear windows had the curtains drawn.

He geared down as he approached the intersection, indicating to turn left a few seconds before Boyle's Peugeot got there.

From her vantage point Tracy watched the impending move unfold just metres away. She was tense with nervous anticipation, but the plan was clear in her mind. She had been impressed with Archer's planning and decision making, and also impressed with how he sold it to Matthew. The Kiwi seemed to have a chip on his shoulder but he was clearly no fool.

In the distance she heard another noise and glanced up. The beat of rotors from a helicopter, maybe a klick out.

The Irishman saw the van in plenty of time and flicked on his right blinker, glancing left as he slowed for the junction. He glanced back to the right as the Kombi started to turn and he clocked the anti-nuke signs and the small Dutch flag stuck on the dash.

Feckin' beatniks.

He glanced up and clocked the driver. Chequered cheese cutter, dark thermal top. Thirties, unshaven.

Tracy realised the heli was on a beeline for them, and at the same time she saw another vehicle approaching from behind Boyle. A maroon Range Rover just coming into sight around the bends, probably half a klick away. No, two maroon Range Rovers. Even from that distance she could see they were both loaded up with passengers.

'Got company, unsure if they're friendlies. Two Rangeys at twelve o'clock.'

———

Boyle felt a tingle at the base of his neck. The driver somehow didn't fit with the van. His right hand began to reach for the Browning.

———

The beat of the rotors got louder, and a man could be seen leaning out the back behind the pilot. The heli looked like a Bell, red markings on white, but Tracy couldn't be sure.

———

Archer saw Boyle's hand move and his body tense up, and knew he'd been burned.

So much for the subtle tap.

He hit the gas and the Kombi leaped forward, T-boning the Peugeot straight in the driver's door. Boyle's side window shattered and the Kombi's engine roared, tyres screaming as the Peugot was shunted sideways.

Tracy saw the heli's nose lift as the pilot powered back and slowed, watching the events below. She could see now that the rear passenger had an M4 in his hands. She hit the switch on her thumb.

'Got an M4 in the heli; watching.'

Her task was to cover Archer, and if it went south she was to take our Boyle. The heli had just thrown a huge spanner in the works.

Archer leaped from the van and discarded the cheese cutter hat. He darted to the Peugeot, which had stalled and flicked round to face him. He only had a couple of seconds to get Boyle under control and had to trust Tracy to cover his arse while he did so. The Irishman was dazed but moving, blood running from his forehead. Archer bounded over the Peugeot's bonnet and reached through the shattered side window, grabbing the terrorist's right arm with one hand and landing a solid hook to the temple with the other.

Boyle's head bounced and he dropped the Browning. Archer seized him by armpits and yanked him up into the window frame of the stoved-in door. The other man groaned and tried to speak. Archer ignored it and dragged him from the car, dumping him on the ground on his front. He quickly looped flexi-cuffs round the terrorist's wrists and yanked them tight.

Tracy maintained a bead on the heli pilot, leaving Archer to do his thing.

Who are these guys? Not cops.

Even as Tracy tried to answer her own question the heli's nose dipped and it swooped in, the gunman in the rear opening up with the M4. She hesitated a split second and the opportunity as lost. Rounds stitched across the Peugeot and through the front of the Kombi van, blowing glass and shrapnel over the road. Archer crouched over his captive, the noise deafeningly loud as the heli buzzed overhead.

'Hit it!' he bellowed, not bothering with the radio now. He snatched the stubby HK MP5K from under his arm, unhooking it from the bungy harness it was attached to so it was free in his hand.

The heli disappeared behind them and Tracy flipped onto her back, scrambling round to get an eyeball. She could hear it still there somewhere, turning to come in for another run. She took a knee, the G3 coming into her shoulder as she scanned for the target.

Suddenly it was above them again and even as she triggered a short burst she knew she'd missed.

Archer threw a look up as he hustled Boyle past the Kombi towards the St Ives road and saw the heli directly above them, the rear gunman leaning out with a grenade in his hand. The cylinder arced towards them, quickly followed by a second, and the heli lifted again.

'Grenade!' Archer shoved Boyle off the side of the road and dived after him, losing the K as he hit the ground but clamping his hands over his ears and remembering to keep his mouth half open and his eyes shut.

The pair of stun grenades went off almost simultaneously, the flash of the magnesium blindingly bright and the thunderous bangs deafening. Archer hit the ground and rolled, keeping his hands in place and his eyes shut until he came to a stop in the ditch at the roadside. Looking up he saw the heli flaring ten metres off the ground, the gunman still hanging out, the M4 back in his hands, checking to see the effect of the flash bangs.

Archer snatched the Sig P228 from his waistband and snapped off a double tap at the gunman, going wide but making the guy flinch enough to send his own burst wide too. By the time the M4 barrel swung back on line Archer was on his knees and firing again, a sustained burst of semi auto fire that punctured the side of the heli and winged the gunman. He yelped and fell back into the cabin as the heli started to lift away.

At the same time as Archer was engaging the rear gunman Tracy rose to her feet, letting the ghillie fall away as she shouldered the G3. The heli was hovering barely twenty metres away and only slightly higher than the ridge she was on. The pilot saw her movement and glanced left, his jaw dropping as he saw the camo-clad figure with a suppressed assault rifle aiming into his cockpit.

She saw his lips move as he shouted a warning to his lone passenger, and she saw the passenger fall back, dropping his M4 and clutching at his arm, presumably hit by Archer down below.

The heli lifted sharply but Tracy had a bead on the pilot and it was too late. She squeezed the trigger, pumping three rounds into the side window with enough force to blow it in, the next three rounds shattering an instrument panel above the pilot's head. He ducked and swerved, the next two bursts stitching holes in the side panels as the heli banked right and tried to escape the auto fire.

As the tail swung round towards Tracy she coolly shifted her aim and cut loose at the tail rotor. High velocity 7.62mm rounds pinged off the steel and the rotor snapped away, throwing the heli into an immediate spin.

Both operators saw it happen and dived to the ground again, covering their heads. The heli spun wildly for nearly fifty metres before it tipped, the rotors clipping the ground first and flinging into the air before the machine hit the deck and bounced, flames immediately licking out.

The second impact brought a devastating explosion and a fireball burst towards the sky.

Archer was up first, grabbing Boyle by the scruff of the neck and snatching up the K before racing towards the RV. Looking over his shoulder he could see the Rangeys now, motoring towards the crash site, both vehicles bristling with weapons.

'Move, fucko.' He hustled Boyle onwards down the narrow winding road until they came to a farm track which disappeared up over a ridge. They took it, cresting the rise in time to see Tracy burst out from beneath a crop of trees in the Saab, camo netting still trailing from the bumper. She skidded to a halt beside them and popped the boot.

Boyle was starting to get his senses back when he was bundled into the boot and the lid was slammed down, leaving him in darkness with a thumping headache and ringing ears.

'Fuck you you goddamn sons of bitches!' he bellowed, kicking at the car seat behind him. 'When I get my hands on you I'll gut you like a goddamn fish and dance on yer feckin' grave, you hear me?'

The boot popped again and Archer leaned in, a cotton swab in his hand. Boyle spat at him and tried to twist away, but within seconds the pad was over his mouth and nose and he was inhaling chloroform. Blackness took over again and the boot slammed down.

Tracy gunned it down the track towards the road, and Archer was just about to comment that the car wrecks should slow the opposition down a while when they both heard the roar of V8 engines approaching.

Archer yanked on his seatbelt and grabbed the G3 from the foot well where Tracy had stashed it, checking the magazine and flicking the safety off. They were nearly at the road when the first rounds hit, pinging off the bodywork and skimming across the windscreen. Looking past Tracy, he could see the first Rangey had stopped just past the crash site and two of the passengers were leaning over the bonnet, sniping at them.

He heard a curse from Tracy and the Saab skidded, slewing almost sideways across the track before coming to a stop.

He turned to see why they weren't moving and clocked the crazed windscreen. He brought his foot up and kicked out, punching a hole through it but managing to pull the glass free of the frame. He twisted and smashed it with his rifle butt, tossing it forward, and Tracy hammered the accelerator.

The Saab fishtailed, bumping heavily over a pot hole and crashing Archer's head into the roof, the tires scrambling for traction on the mud and gravel. Fire came from their right again, the car thudding with hits, but she was into the mouth of the track now and the car crashed sideways into a fence post.

There was a screech of tortured metal as the back panel was ripped free by the post, then they were onto the road and the tires were smoking on the tarmac as Tracy gassed it.

'Stop stop stop!' Archer shouted and threw his door open. Tracy braked without question and he leaped out, the G3 coming on line and sighting at the three gunmen he could see running forwards from the first Rangey. They all had their ski masks down and were firing as they ran, the rush of adrenaline making their decision a poor one; they had left cover and their fire was ineffective.

Archer crouched and triggered a three-round burst at them, dropping one, pumped another couple of bursts and made the other two dive for cover, then turned towards the Rangey. He aimed for the radiator and fired a volley of rounds at it. Nothing, and he was taking incoming fire. Tracy was screaming at him to get back in as he ripped off another burst at the gunmen then emptied his mag at the petrol tank.

Nothing happened for a second then, as he leaped back into the Saab, the Rangey exploded with a roar. A plume of fire shot skywards and debris flew in all directions, pinging off the road as they raced away. Archer grinned at Tracy as he dropped the G3's empty mag and inserted a full one, working the bolt to chamber a round.

She had several pin pricks of blood on her face from the flying glass and a lock of hair had come loose, falling over her face. Her hands were white knuckled on the wheel. Despite all this, she had a glow that he recognised.

'Who the fuck were those guys?' she shouted. Wind whistled through the car and one of the wheels was making a knocking noise. They were both deafened from the shooting.

'I dunno. Looked maybe Iraqi.' He turned and looked behind them. The second Range Rover was approaching at speed from beyond the black smoke pouring from the burning Rangey. 'And here come some more!'

Tracy floored it and Archer kept an eye on the following enemy, seeing the second Rangey slow long enough for the remaining two original gunmen to jump aboard. It came after them again and he sat back down, grabbing his cell phone out and checking the screen. It was on silent, and he saw three missed calls and a voice message from Rob Moore.

He ignored them and hit the fast dial for Matthew Livingstone. Livingstone was in an Ops Room back at Fort Monckton, waiting for an update.

He answered immediately with, 'You're on speaker, go ahead.'

Archer clamped the phone to his ear and shouted over the ambient noise. 'We've got the package but we got bumped by a hit team, Middle Easterns, with M4s.'

'Casualties?' Livingstone's voice had a calm urgency.

'None for us, three of them and a vehicle down. We've got a carload of them chasing us now, probably another half dozen or so. Our car's fucked. We're heavily outnumbered and outgunned.' There was silence down the line and Archer thought he'd missed the reply due to his temporary deafness. 'What?'

'Stand by,' Livingstone came back tersely.

Archer checked behind again. The Rangey was gaining, probably three hundred and fifty metres back now. He looked at Tracy who was scowling at the instrument panel.

'The turbo's fucked,' she shouted, 'it's not kicking in. We're overheating too and the oil light's on.' She slammed the wheel with the palm of her hand. 'Come on baby, be good for mama.'

Archer grinned despite himself.

Livingstone came back on the line. 'I don't know who the unfriendlies are. I presume they're possibly Saudis. It doesn't change the plan. I'm sorry, but there is no support for you.'

'The boys at Poole could be here in twenty minutes,' Archer yelled, referring to the Special Boat Service of the Royal Marines. They were the naval Special Forces unit, less known but equally as competent as their Army peers.

'No,' Livingstone came back quickly. 'You're on your own. Whatever you do, don't let them get the package.' He paused. 'If needs be, close the package down.'

Archer scowled in frustration. 'If you want us to kill him, just fuckin' say so,' he snarled. 'We'll see you back there for afternoon tea.'

He disconnected and shoved the phone in his pocket, getting onto his knees again and leaning into the backseat.

'I take it we're flying solo?' Tracy enquired as Archer secured their weapons.

'Yep. Could be a long day.'

30

The road was empty and windy with minimal tree cover now as they came more into rugged farmland than forest.

Archer could see the Rangey still making ground. His mind was racing trying to work out their next moves. The car was obviously on its last legs, they were in the middle of nowhere and the unknown enemy seemed determined to bring the fight to them despite their early losses.

Just then the car started slowing and Tracy swore angrily. 'The fucker's dead.'

They coasted to a stop and Archer bailed out, sighting through the G3's scope at the approaching Rangey. There was a sweeping curve between them, making it only about two hundred metres as the crow flew to the target. He'd made plenty of harder shots than that before.

He leaned into a stable shooting stance and cracked a shot at the Rangey, hitting the windscreen dead centre. The Rangey swerved to the wrong side of the road and his next shot blew the front passenger's window in.

He handed the weapon to Tracy at his side. 'Swap it to HE.'

She quickly replaced the smoke canister in the breech of the

HK79 with a 40mm high explosive round. She snapped the launcher closed and handed the weapon back, taking the HK machine pistol and swapping spare magazines with him.

Archer pointed back towards the car. 'Get him out,' he said, 'take cover past the car and get ready to move. I'll keep these fuck-knuckles at bay and give you a shout to move. I'll catch you up.'

She jumped to it and he shouldered the G3 again, seeing the Rangey had stopped at the shoulder and a couple of shooters had debussed, taking up positions at each end of the vehicle. Rounds started coming overhead and he could see they were slightly lower down in a dip, so were shooting up at angle.

He dropped to a knee to minimise his profile and plinked a shot at the tail end shooter. The guy ducked back when the taillight exploded in front of him. Archer moved to the shooter leaning across the bonnet, and put a round through the sheet metal at his elbow, causing him to jump back and juggle his rifle with fright. Archer's next shot took him square in the chest and knocked him back against the stone wall, dropping his weapon.

The Rangey jerked backwards and the fallen gunman was exposed. Archer could see him clutching at his chest and gasping for breath, winded by the impact on his armour. Archer sighted carefully and let out his breath, stroking the trigger smoothly. The big rifle bucked in his grip and the gunman's head popped like a melon hitting the pavement.

The Rangey shot backwards with the far side passenger's door open, the second shooter being dragged in by his mates.

'Move!' Archer called out, 'I'll catch you up.'

Behind him Tracy popped the boot and was relieved to see that Boyle was alive and didn't appear to have even taken a scratch, despite the volume of fire they'd just been through.

She hefted the unconscious terrorist over her shoulder in a fireman's carry, staggering at first as he was heavier than she'd expected. She already had the weight of her holstered Sig plus a grab bag of emergency supplies slung across body with the MP5K jammed into it. She sucked in a breath, steadied herself and started off at a trot.

The Rangey pulled back fifty metres and stopped around a bend. Archer knew they would be regrouping and talking tactics. Unless they were highly trained, he had about a minute. He backed up to the car and confirmed that Tracy had taken what she should have.

He left the remaining gear behind and took the second grab bag, before vaulting the stone wall into a paddock. A few sheep were grazing on the far side, oblivious to the goings-on around them. He could partially see the Rangey from the new position. He dug out a water bottle for a quick drink while he took stock and caught his breath.

The G3 had four full magazines left and he had a dozen rounds for the HK-79 in his Molle belt. Tracy had four full mags for the K. With five or six well-armed and determined enemy hunting them, every shot had to count. Distance was the key for now, which meant he had to even the odds.

He spotted Tracy at the far side of the next paddock, swinging a leg over the stone wall with Boyle over her shoulder. His admiration for her toughness rose a notch further. He still couldn't quite believe she'd shot down a helicopter.

Scanning back towards the enemy he saw the rear doors open and three guys piled out, running across the road towards the stone wall bordering the paddocks there. Each was carrying an M4.

Good; no sniper weapons.

Archer gauged they were about two hundred and fifty metres from him now, giving him a decent buffer from the short-barrelled M4s. He hadn't seen a scope on any of the rifles and it was unlikely any of them would have the skills to hit him at that range on iron sights. The G3's scope and heavier calibre gave him a distinct advantage now, even without his own skills.

He figured there were at least two guys left in the Rangey, most likely including the commander. Archer began working his way forward, rolling over the stone walls and crossing the paddocks until he figured he was about a hundred metres away. The camber of the ground afforded some protection. He knew the three enemy would be moving slower with having to climb the bank at the side of the road first, and would be wary of his sniping.

He carefully checked over the wall in front of him, seeing a shooter jumping the wall two paddocks away. A quick peek through a gap in the side wall showed the Rangey about eighty metres away, parked on the shoulder of the road with the engine running.

Archer readied the HK-79, adjusting the sights and carefully calculating the angle. He worked a rock loose to widen the gap he'd found and took aim.

The grenade sailed through the air and landed directly in front of the Rangey, exploding with a roar and throwing the front of the wagon off the ground. He slipped a second HE round into the chamber and took aim again, seeing both front doors open as the occupants tried to escape.

The second grenade went through the windscreen and blew all the windows and doors out, engulfing the two shooters in flames. Archer reloaded as the Rangey exploded with a thunderous bang and roar of flames. Pieces of shrapnel scattered and black smoke billowed skyward.

He rose above the wall and spotted two of the shooters standing and watching the carnage as if dumbfounded. The third was looking in his direction and shouted a warning, unleashing a volley of fire that threw up tufts of grass in the paddock metres in front of Archer.

The G3 spat fire back, a three round burst blowing chunks of stone off the wall in front of the three enemy. They dropped from sight and Archer crabbed to his right, taking up a new position near the middle of the wall. He readied the 79 again and sent a grenade their way.

It exploded behind them and he heard a scream. Wild rifle fire erupted as they panicked and he gave them a couple of seconds before launching his next grenade, dropping it neatly behind them as they bolted back across the paddock, two of them dragging the third between them.

The concussion knocked them off their feet and he saw one of them grabbing at his leg, peppered with shrapnel. The third shooter got to his feet and ran, abandoning his comrades. Archer brought the G3 up and watched the man hurl himself over the next wall.

A second later he could be seen still sprinting away, his rifle discarded. Archer contemplated for a second then snugged the rifle butt against his cheek. He sighted on the man who was now a good two hundred metres away, slowed his breathing and let it out, waiting.

As the shooter reached the next stone wall he put both hands on top and vaulted, swinging his legs up to the right. A 7.62mm round shattered his left hip and he was thrown forward, landing in a screaming heap. He possibly wouldn't die, which was okay. If he didn't then two things would result; the security services or Police would get a chance to have a crack at him, and he would automatically be a liability to his employer – a liability that might force them into doing something silly.

Archer turned and ran, faintly hearing sirens in the far distance. Presumably a farmer had heard all the action and called at least the fire service but probably the cops as well. They needed to move.

He paused to toss a white phosphorous grenade into the Saab as he passed, and it exploded behind him as he made ground to catch up to Tracy and Boyle.

They were hunkered down in a clump of undergrowth when he caught up. Tracy's top was stained with sweat and she was sucking in deep breaths through her nose. She paused to take a long draught of water as Archer joined them.

Boyle was stirring, finally waking from his drugged stupor. He slowly focussed and shifted his gaze from one to the other, his teeth pulling back into a snarl as he recognised them. He started to speak, then retched and vomited on his own lap. He brought up a second deposit then flopped back, panting and swearing at them through a thick tongue.

Archer poured some water in his face and mouth, and started to roll him onto his side so he didn't choke. Boyle spat the dirty water back in his face with a sneer and tried to buck at him. Tracy quickly dropped a knee on his back and held him down while Archer reapplied the chloroform pad, holding it tight until Boyle stopped thrashing again and went back to sleep.

'Not sure how many times you can do that,' Archer commented, putting the pack away. He shrugged. 'Oh well.'

He handed her the rifle and mags. While he hefted the prisoner onto his shoulder Tracy dialled Livingstone again. The conversation was short and a minute later a text bleeped on her phone, giving them map co-ordinates for an RV. Archer tramped on, constantly scanning the surrounds while she navigated. Three columns of smoke spiralled up behind them, providing an easy guide for the emergency services that he was certain would be blue-lighting there, if they were not on site already.

The sun was up now and Boyle was a dead weight, one that stunk of sweat and vomit. He tried to block out the discomfort and concentrate on getting some distance between them and the scene of the fire-fight.

'About three miles,' Tracy said from behind him. 'Keep straight and aim for that stone shed at one o'clock.'

The sound of rotors came across the farmland and Tracy spotted an incoming heli.

'Cover!'

They made it to a small dip and tucked down, covering their heads and hoping they hadn't been seen. The heli, which bore the coastguard colours, flew by and headed towards the scene a couple of miles back without appearing to have seen them.

They were up and moving again within seconds, beset with a sense of real urgency now. If they were caught with the weapons and a drugged prisoner, Archer had no doubt the Government – both of them, for that matter – would deny any knowledge and they would be facing a lengthy jail sentence.

He dug it in, concentrating on one step at a time, pounding across the rough ground with the M-79 bumping against his thigh and Boyle's dead weight pressing down into his shoulder and neck. Tracy kept them on track and within half an hour they were less than a mile from the RV point.

Tracy dug out her phone and sent a text update to Livingstone, without getting a reply. As he maintained the steady pace Archer couldn't shake the thought that they were playing behind the eight ball. Whoever the ambushers had been – Iraqi? Saudi? Iranian? – they had known Boyle's movements. Their attack was not something thrown together at the last minute, and he and Tracy had been bloody lucky to get out alive.

Whoever those guys were, they either had as good intel as the spooks, or they had another way of tracking Boyle. And what was their motivation? Kill him? Capture him? The use of flash bangs rather than frags indicated the latter – but why?

Archer shifted the thought aside for now; it was too much to think about and he needed to keep his wits about him until they'd handed over their prisoner and got the hell out of Dodge.

He dug it in up a rise, and sensed Tracy move up alongside him.

'Other side of this rise,' she said, 'less than half a klick to go.'

'Great,' he grunted, 'this prick stinks.'

Tracy went ahead and crawled to the lip of the rise, doing a visual clearance before waving Archer forward.

31

They crested the rise cautiously and dropped down into a small valley.

A long track led from a farm road to a barn that stood with the doors closed. As they got nearer Archer could see fresh tyre tracks on the path and one of the doors opened slightly.

When they got to the doors a guy in jeans, a long coat and an earpiece opened the door and let them in, sliding a bolt across behind them. He had a Walther MPL sub machine gun front-slung, and looked like he knew how to use it. A similar looking character stood in the loft on the far side of the barn, watching out through a small vent.

Two Fords were parked in the middle of the barn, the closest one a dark blue Transit van with tinted windows, a plain red Mondeo sedan behind it.

Matthew Livingstone appeared from behind the van, a wide grin on his face.

'Well done,' he said, sticking out his hand to shake Tracy's. 'Safe and secure?'

Archer grunted and dumped Boyle unceremoniously on the dirty floor. 'As safe and secure as we can be with a hunter force after us and all the cops in the district scouring the countryside, yeah.'

Livingstone brushed the comment aside and extended his hand. Archer reluctantly shook it. It was soft and moist and he released the grip quickly.

'No problem,' Livingstone said breezily, 'we'll take care of it from here. You two get yourselves tidied up and back to London. We'll speak later.'

The spotter up the top shimmied down a ladder and helped his colleague shift Boyle into the back of the Transit. The terrorist was stirring again, and without warning vomited on the hands of the closest heavy. The guy didn't say a word – neither of them had yet spoken – just wiped his hands carefully on Boyle's jacket and continued shifting him.

They placed him in a single seat that was bolted to the floor with his back against the side wall. They cut the cable ties and strapped him into the seat by the arms and ankles. A matching seat faced it, and one of the heavies took a position there.

Boyle was awake properly now, and turned to look at his captors. He sneered at Archer and Tracy. 'We'll meet again,' he said, his tone thick with venom, 'and we'll see who's laughin' then, shall we?'

'Nobody's laughing mate, 'Archer replied evenly, 'although you are a fuckin' joke.'

'Save it,' Livingstone cut in, shutting the rear doors as Boyle launched into a stream of obscenities. He indicated for the second heavy to get in and handed a set of keys to Tracy. 'It's one of ours,' he said, 'just drop it back in the pool when you get back.' He turned to go but Archer stopped him with a hand on the arm.

'Hold up there, doctor,' he said, and Livingstone raised an eyebrow. Archer ushered them both away from the van to avoid eavesdropping. 'You've got a problem.'

'My problem is that we should be on the road by now.'

'No, your problem is that whoever bumped us has just as good intel as you do. Maybe better.'

There was silence for a few moments as Livingstone took that in. 'It is concerning that these guys turned up,' he agreed.

'It's more than concerning, mate,' Archer retorted. 'As far as I can see it means either you've got a leak somewhere or that crew – whoever they are – are dialled into him somehow. I don't know how, but I'm guessing it means either they have an informant like you guys do, or they've gone electronic on him.'

Tracy nodded in agreement but said nothing. It confused Archer that despite her obvious skills and cool head in the field, she was still intimidated by a pasty office guy in a suit.

'I'm thinking they must be electronic,' Livingstone finally said, staring at a spot over Archer's shoulder as he thought aloud. 'Our systems are pretty damn robust, so I doubt we have a leak.' He held his hands up placatingly as Archer opened his mouth to protest. 'But I will look into it. Trust me, I will.' He smiled again and touched them each on the arm. 'You two get away now and rest up, it's been a hell of a day for you. We'll need to debrief later.'

He adopted a serious tone. 'Sincerely guys, the Firm owes you a big thank you. Boyle's a very bad man who needs to be off the streets.' He nodded to them and headed to the van.

Archer opened the barn doors long enough to let them out before shedding all his gear into the boot of the Mondeo. Tracy opened a water bottle and was about to start washing her face when Archer stopped her.

'In a minute,' he told her firmly. 'Sort out your weapons first, then your gear, then yourself. Right?'

She pulled a face. 'Man, you're a squaddie through and through aren't you?'

'And it's kept me alive so far.' He cleared his weapons and made them safe, keeping the Sig in his waistband for now.

Tracy followed suit and they secured the longs in the boot. Their grab bags were emptied of food and water and also stashed, along with their dirtied jackets. Tracy located a pair of hoodies in the front seat, which they donned before quickly washing off the obvious dirt and grime from their exposed skin.

Archer took the wheel and they left the barn behind, guzzling water and necking the food rations they had – chocolate, muesli bars and trail mix. Within a few minutes they were onto a decent road and heading north.

They could see a couple of heli's still up a few miles away and Archer was concerned they would be caught in a roadblock. When they got near Hayle they found a checkpoint being set up, but the pair of officers were still putting cones out and not paying attention, so Archer cruised on past without incident. Soon they were on the A30 and making good time. Archer expected Tracy to be exhausted but she seemed to be agitated instead. Her face was pinched tight and she was staring fixedly out the side window.

All of a sudden she dry retched and put a hand to her mouth, waving at him with the other hand. Archer slid to the shoulder and braked hard, seeing her door open before the car had even stopped.

He sat and avoided staring while she threw up. After a few minutes she sat back and shut the door, wiping her nose and mouth.

'Alright?'

She nodded, not looking at him. He slipped the car into gear and got moving. The hum of the road filled the Mondeo until he spoke again.

'Don't worry about it,' he said softly, 'it happens to the best of us.'

Tracy said nothing, just stared at the passing countryside.

'First time up close?'

She nodded slightly and glanced quickly at him then away again.

'My first time wasn't too flash. It was messy and scary and confusing.' He shook his head at the memory. 'It just wasn't pleasant.'

Tracy turned back to the front now, tucking her hands under her thighs. 'What d'you mean, confusing?'

He thought for a moment before responding. 'A lot of noise and action. And it was very quick.'

'Not confusing then as in you weren't sure...' Her voice trailed off and she went back to staring out the window.

Archer let her be and concentrated on driving. He was tired and achy and keen to get back to the hotel. Suddenly Tracy turned in her seat and spoke again.

'So it's not unpleasant anymore?'

'What?'

'You said your first time was not pleasant. Is it pleasant now?' Her tone was almost accusing. 'Do you enjoy it now?'

Archer frowned and carefully considered his answer. 'No, it's not pleasant. It's not pleasant like a good meal or an enjoyable occasion. It's satisfying to survive.' He frowned at her. 'And it's satisfying to know you've done a good job.'

Tracy's brow furrowed into lines and she pursed her lips.

'It's not wrong to think that,' he said harshly. 'We all play the game and we all want to win, but someone has to lose. You just hope to God it's not you.' He looked back to the front again, scowling now. 'And if it is, well...you just make sure you take some of the bastards with you.'

'Well I think we managed to do that today, don't you?' she said, still turned away.

'We did what we needed to do. They brought the fight to us; we didn't go looking for it.' Archer was speaking through gritted teeth now. 'They got what was coming to them.'

'Huh.' Tracy snorted derisively. 'That's a very cold way of looking at it. I saw you, the way you were...excited. Like a schoolboy playing war with his mates, all *Boy's Own Adventure*.' Her eyes were hot as she glared at him. 'Only some of them didn't walk away.'

'Who gives a fuck?' Archer braked hard again and jerked the car into a lay-by, stopping quickly as he turned in his seat to face her. 'Honestly, who gives a shit if those pricks got taken out? They were fuckin' terrorists and our job is to beat them at their own game. They ambushed us, we fought back and got away, and killed some of them in the process. So fuckin' what? They're evil cunts and the world's a better place today. I for one won't lose a wink of sleep over them.' He held her angry stare before shaking his head in frustration. 'You did good back there so I don't know what you're so shitty about.'

'I'm not shitty,' she fired back hotly.

'Well if you can't handle it then you better fuck off back to being a spook and leave the dirty work to the big boys,' he snarled. 'I can't work with you if you're going to break down afterwards.'

Tracy's hand shot out and he caught it by the wrist a hair's breadth from his cheek. They glared at each other as they both strained. Finally Tracy relented and eased back.

'I'm not shitty,' she said softly, 'I was just scared. I killed two guys today and I don't know how I should be feeling about it.' She shook her head gently. 'I'm not shitty.'

Archer studied her quietly. 'It's normal,' he said, 'just let it ride. You'll be fine.'

She gave a small nod and started to turn away again. Archer put his hand on her arm and she paused. 'Look at me, Tracy.'

She reluctantly turned towards him, her eyes slowly lifting to his face.

'You'll be fine,' he said, giving her a reassuring nod. 'You will be.'

She gave the small nod again and turned back in her seat. He could see the tension in her shoulders release a notch. 'And I can't believe you took down a helicopter,' he added.

'What?'

'You just blew a bloody chopper out of the sky, as cool and calm as you like. If that's not , I don't know what is.'

Tracy rolled her eyes at him and smiled now. She punched him on the arm. 'You're a shit.'

He rolled back onto the A30 and headed north.

32

Steam filled the shower cubicle as Archer let the jets wash away the grime and blood and sweat.

His body was sore from the enforced march with Boyle over his shoulder and he was wondering if he would have time for a good hard sports massage tomorrow.

He knew a great place off Charing Cross Road run by Koreans who weren't great conversationalists but certainly knew how to get the kinks out. Maybe it's not such a good idea anymore, he mused as he washed his hair for the second time. They're probably bloody spies.

The more he saw of his new world, the more he realised it was like a parallel universe. All sorts of seemingly normal people doing very strange things, moving alongside normal people who were living their everyday lives and completely oblivious to the goings on around them.

Smoke and mirrors, Jedi had said. Well, he wasn't wrong.

Archer stepped out and vigorously towelled himself dry. He took his time shaving and examined his bumps and bruises before dressing; nothing to worry about. Officers had cleaned out his hotel room while he and Tracy debriefed with a senior spook, and his luggage had been placed in quarters at Legoland.

He hadn't been surprised to learn they had barracks-like accommodation on site as well, which seemed to be furnished from a charity shop and smelled of farts. He sat on the single bed and dressed slowly, dumped his dirty gear in a plastic bag for washing and repacked his luggage.

Freshly dressed in jeans and a shirt with the tails out, Archer made his way upstairs to the cafeteria. He'd been issued a pass which had very limited access, and the spook that had debriefed them told him to hang around for the day while they sorted a few things out and arranged a new hotel.

Archer presumed that the few things including trying to bleed Boyle dry of intel.

The cafe was nearly empty after the lunchtime rush, just a couple of girls finishing up coffees and a young Asian guy sitting alone and playing Angry Birds on his phone.

Remember it's Asian, not Paki; you're in England now.

The two girls glanced at him as he entered then did a double take as if realising who he was. He ignored them and ordered a coffee from the fat black woman behind the counter. The two girls were still looking when he turned to scout a seat. He gave them a smile and moved to the far side of the cafe where soft armchairs looked out over the Thames.

He flicked through a well-thumbed copy of the morning's Times while he waited for his coffee. It arrived at the same time as his phone bleeped with an incoming message. It was Rob Moore and the message was to the point.

Call me.

Moore answered immediately. 'You across the river?' His tone was urgent.

'Yeah. Waiting to be kicked out.'

'Free to speak?'

'Yeah, are you? I was trying to get hold of you. You didn't answer.'

'Yeah well I've been tied up for about eighteen fuckin' hours with my American friend.'

Archer was silent as he waited.

'Anything you wanna tell me about that?' Moore said testily.

'If you've been talking to him for that long you can probably figure it out for yourself.'

'Might've been nice to know before I started to get my arse chewed off, mate.'

'How about you tell your mate to keep a better eye on his troops then and shit like that won't happen.' Archer was tired and losing patience now. 'They were off the reservation and trying to do a number on me.' He took a breath to calm down. 'I tried to tell you.'

The line was silent but he could sense Moore seething at the other end.

'They're not happy.'

'I couldn't care less, mate. They need to sort their shit out before they come crying to you. What game are they playing anyway?'

'They weren't,' Moore snapped. 'Those guys weren't on their books any more. They must've been private.'

Archer paused. That put a different spin on things. 'What about the cops?'

'A deal gone wrong. Gangland stuff. The Friends have had a word.'

Jesus, is every spy agency involved in this thing?

Archer sipped his coffee. It was scalding hot and bitter. 'So nobody needs to speak to me then.'

'Huh.' Moore grunted. 'No, but a heads up would've been nice.'

'I tried –'

'I know, I know. I was at a meet first then when that finished I was straight into sorting this out.'

'Sorry mate,' Archer said, although he wasn't entirely convinced he should be apologising. 'I'll try harder next time.'

Moore gave a short laugh. 'Or even better...'

Archer saw Tracy enter the cafe and head in his direction. 'Gotta go mate, I'll catch up with you later.' He disconnected and put the phone away as she took the seat opposite him.

Her hair was still wet from the shower and she'd changed into a charcoal pant suit and a sharp white shirt. The two girls headed back to the office, whispering to each other as they did so.

Archer indicated them with a flick of the chin. 'Do I have food on my face or something?'

Tracy grinned. 'Big news like this doesn't happen every day,' she said. 'Everyone's talking about it. The Director even called me personally to congratulate me on the coup, as she put it.'

Archer gave an approving smile. 'Nice one.' He noticed she had the spark back in her eye. 'You seem pretty chirpy.'

She grinned again. 'The boss has even approved a blank expense claim for us. She told me to take our Antipodean friend out for a nice dinner and show him what London has to offer.'

'Well, there's one person who still uses that term,' he grinned.

'So, let's go.'

33

The restaurant Tracy chose was near Victoria, hidden away in a cobbled alley with a discreet sign beside the heavy oak door. Archer didn't catch the name of it and didn't care; he was hungry and had more than food on his mind as he watched Tracy's sculpted backside move in front of him.

They were quickly seated at a corner table covered with stark white linen. The ceiling was low with heavy exposed beams. The candle in the wrought iron stick in the centre of the table flickered and threw dancing shadows on the stone walls.

The waiter gave them a wine list and went to leave. Archer stopped him short.

'Glenfiddich on the rocks please,' he said, giving Tracy a glance. 'For both of us.'

She looked like she was going to protest, but thought better of it. The waiter nodded and disappeared. Tracy cocked an eyebrow.

'I didn't realise our relationship was at that stage, Craig,' she said with the twitch of a smile, 'would you like to order my dinner for me as well?'

He wasn't entirely sure if she was joking. 'Don't go all "independent woman" on me. It's a tradition I instituted with my troop,' he explained. 'After a successful contact we would crack a Glen.'

'I'm not much of a drinker,' she confided.

'I noticed.' He grinned. 'Just be glad I don't make you do the soapbox.'

'Soapbox? Like at Speaker's Corner?'

It was his turn to raise an eyebrow. 'I don't know about Speaker's Corner, but our soapbox was for all newbies to the troop. You'd have to...'

He was interrupted by the return of the waiter with their drinks. Archer waved him away and raised his glass. 'Bottoms up.'

Archer held Tracy's gaze as they drained their tumblers, ensuring she finished it in one hit. The heat of the whisky consumed his throat and down into his belly, a wonderful warm glow setting in after the initial alcoholic kick. Tracy struggled to finish hers but gamely set the empty glass down with a clunk. She wiped her mouth carefully with the back of her hand and let out a low gasp of almost sexual pleasure.

'Wow,' she finally managed, sitting back. 'Mr Archer, I don't think I should make this a regular thing.'

'Drinking?'

'Drinking with you.'

He laughed and handed her the drinks menu. 'Nothing to worry about love, that's it for tonight.' He grinned cheekily. 'Just an ice breaker. You can choose the wine.'

'What, d'you think I'm cultured enough to choose wine in a posh restaurant? I'm from Croydon, nothing posh about that.'

'Yeah well I'm pretty sure you'll be more cultured than a hick from the sticks, so it's all on you.'

The waiter drifted back and they ordered starters and mains in one go; Archer was pleased to see Tracy didn't hold back for once. Tea smoked salmon with lemon and radish for two followed by sea bass with kale and pork belly for Tracy and lamb with turnips, shallot and Lancashire pudding for Archer.

Tracy ordered a bottle of Ronco del Gnemiz Sauvignon Sol from Italy, and looked at Archer as the waiter wafted away again. 'What?'

'Are you serious? That was ninety six quid! Your boss'll have a shit fit.'

She waved a hand airily at him. 'Bahh, don't worry, she won't care. Besides, you should see what she and Matthew put away.' She shook her head in wonderment. 'They'd do this every week, so just enjoy it while you can.'

Archer mentally shrugged and did as he was told. The starter was excellent and he ate with gusto, washing it down with the sweet fruitiness of the Sav. He had always thought white wine should be matched with white meat and fish, but Tracy had a different viewpoint.

'If you're a wine snob, yeah,' she said. 'But I think what you personally like is more important.' She shrugged. 'And I like Italian, so that's what we're having.'

He couldn't argue that and it was good wine with good food, so he topped up their glasses and braced himself for the main. It proved to be just as excellent as the starter and he closed his eyes to savour the full-bodied flavour of the tender lamb. When he opened them, Tracy was looking at him with amusement. Her eyes were smiling and her lips slightly parted, like she knew something naughty and wanted to tell.

'What?' He suddenly felt self conscious and wiped his mouth.

'You're definitely a man who likes his food.' The tip of her tongue flicked across her lower lip. 'It's nice to see.'

'Food should be enjoyed,' he said earnestly. 'I hate seeing people picking and dancing round it like it's something to be scared of. You should be in there with your sleeves rolled up, exploring it and discovering something new every time you take a bite.'

Tracy cocked her eyebrow at him but said nothing. She didn't need to; he could see it in her eyes.

'I love food, I love cooking it and I love eating it.' He leaned forward across the table, looking into her eyes. 'There's something very exciting about sharing a good meal with a woman.'

She gave him that playful smile again. 'The way you describe it, it's almost a sexual thing.'

Archer held her gaze. 'It is. It's very intimate. When you eat you reveal what you like and you show your inner self.' He smiled slightly, still holding her gaze. 'The beast that lurks within must be sated somehow.'

'Sounds like your beast is hungry,' she replied, leaning forward now too. Their faces were scarcely inches apart. Her warm breath made his skin tingle.

'It is,' he agreed. 'I think it needs to be fed.' Tracy still had that twinkle in her eye and he decided to push his luck. *God she's arousing.* 'How's your beast feeling? Satisfied, or wanting more?'

Tracy smiled and he was sure she could hear his heart pounding in his chest, like a teenager on heat. She leaned back and his heart sank.

'I think my beast is okay,' she said gently, still smiling but with a touch of disappointment now.

Archer leaned back too, feeling like a chump. His cheeks burned with embarrassment and he didn't know where to look.

'I'm sorry,' Tracy said softly, 'but I think we eat off different menus, if you know what I mean.'

He looked at her quizzically and it slowly dawned on him. He felt an even bigger fool, but relieved at the same time. 'Oh,' he said. The thought had occurred to him earlier, but her flirtatiousness had dispelled it.

'Don't worry, you haven't lost your touch.' Tracy grinned at him and took a sip of her wine. 'And if I ever go back to your menu, I'll be sure to give you a call.'

He grinned and felt the humiliation start to ebb. 'Please do. But for now, how about dessert?'

Archer ordered praline mousse with white chocolate and muscovado sugar ice cream. Tracy asked the waiter for a second spoon, and when it came she helped herself off his plate. It was a rich and velvety heaven and together they devoured it, savouring every spoonful until the dish had been scraped clean.

They took their time over coffees and Archer started slipping into a contented state with a full belly and a warm glow. He still felt a fool for being spurned, but comforted himself with the thought that he was years too late in that department so it was nothing personal.

He waited while Tracy settled the bill and hailed a cab. She leaned against him as they watched the cab slide to a stop at the kerb.

'Thank you for a lovely evening, Mr Archer,' she smiled, and tiptoed to give him a peck on the cheek. She lingered there for a second before stepping away towards the cab. 'I'm a little bit gutted, but what can you do?'

He shrugged and opened the door for her. 'And thank you too, Ms Spencer.' They grinned at each other and he leaned to give her a brief but firm hug. 'You were magnificent. I'll talk to you tomorrow.'

He shut the door behind her and watched the cab pull away. Tracy waggled her fingers out the back window and he tipped an imaginary hat before turning to hunt out another cab.

He still had an alcohol buzz in his veins and the beast had not been sated.

34

The pub doors closed at eleven sharp and Becky emerged from the staff entrance ten minutes later, her coat flapping at her legs as she hurried up the alley to the footpath.

She was rummaging in her bag when she sensed somebody's presence and looked up. It was the Kiwi guy from the night before, the one who'd promised so much but failed to deliver.

He stood motionless on the footpath, hands in the pockets of his long black coat, a wolfish half smile on his face as he watched her. Becky paused as she sized him up. He wasn't handsome in the classic matinee idol way, but that was fine. His nose had been broken at least once and he had a small scar on the right of his upper lip which gave him an almost-curl when he spoke.

He had the kind of confident rugged appeal of a soldier or fireman. This was no pink shirt-wearing pretty-boy who wanted to talk about his feelings or debate climate change. This was a man's man who knew what he wanted and was going to take charge.

A thrill ran through her.

'Alright?' she said nonchalantly, giving him disinterested.

The Kiwi smiled, his eyes warm and strong as they searched her face. 'I feel bad.'

'That you ran out last night?'

'It wasn't nice.' He stepped closer to her and she could smell his aftershave, something deep and warm and masculine. Becky let the smell fill her nostrils. 'I usually have impeccable manners.'

'Really?' She cocked her head up at him. 'All the time?'

'Well.' He gave a tiny twitch of the head. 'Not all the time.'

'I hope not.' Becky took another step, into his personal space now. 'Sometimes a bad boy can be just what the doctor ordered.' Another step brought them torso to torso. Neither backed off. 'And I'm feeling a bit poorly. I may need a lie down.'

Archer smiled down at her, feeling her press against him. 'Enough talk,' he said softly.

She proved to be as adventurous in bed as he had anticipated, throwing herself into it with an enthusiasm he admired. She was voluptuous and womanly in every way and knew what she wanted. He gave it to her and she willingly returned it with interest, and when they finally collapsed on the tangled sheets of his hotel bed, he was exhausted.

Becky rolled over in the darkness and reached for her watch on the floor. 'Plenty of time for a shower,' she said, rolling back to Archer. She ran her fingers through his chest hair, down to his stomach, and down again.

He looked at her quizzically. 'Really?'

'Really.'

She was certainly determined to get the most out of the night, so he went with it and afterwards they showered together, washing the sweat and sex off each other's bodies. Becky stepped out of the shower first and towelled herself dry in front of the mirror. She had a wide tattoo across her lower back, some kind of scroll design. A small red rose adorned her left shoulder blade. Archer cut the water and drew back the curtain, standing naked and wet as he watched her.

She looked at him in the reflection, unashamed of her nakedness. 'I should be getting home,' she said.

He stepped out of the shower and stood behind her, pressing his body against hers. His hands came around to cup her full breasts, his fingers lightly brushing her nipples.

She let out a small gasp. 'That isn't helping me get ready.' She pressed back against him, feeling his excitement.

'Oh, I think it is.' He continued what he was doing for a few moments and she responded by reaching down and guiding him into her again.

It was nearly three when she finally left the hotel room, checking her watch again and cursing.

'Somebody expecting you home?' Archer asked lazily from the bed. She hadn't mentioned anyone else, but then he hadn't bothered asking either; that was her business.

'My sister's lookin' after the kids. She'll kill me.' Becky hurriedly closed her bag and leaned over the bed for a last kiss, firm and hot. 'Hope I see y'round, Kiwi boy. Don't be a stranger now.'

She gave him that cheeky grin and opened the door, throwing a shaft of light into the room from the hallway. Archer gave her a smile and a wave and she was gone. The room fell into darkness again and he lay back on the wrecked bed, thinking of Tracy and Jazz and the other women of his life.

It was a trail of broken hearts and unfulfilled promises and it wasn't something he tended to linger on. He rolled over and smiled as he thought of Becky and their brief time together. Sometimes the beast within just had to be fed.

35

The NZ High Commission in Samoa was a yellow stone building on the main street of Apia, not far from their accommodation at the famous Aggie Grey's Hotel. It was home to the usual Government embassy staffers, plus a Police liaison officer and a representative from the SIS.

Archer and Tracy had landed the previous night on a commercial flight, travelling as lovers on an island getaway. He had tried to sleep but was constantly woken by her either giving him interesting facts about the island nation or asking him questions about it. She had a guide book which was far superior to his own limited knowledge. She was fascinated by the idea of *fa'afafine's* and didn't quite get why he wasn't.

They were met at Reception by the resident SIS officer, a small, flabby man in his late thirties with thinning dark hair and a relaxed air. He shook hands and introduced himself as Jonty, before escorting them into an office on the ground floor. The desk was scattered with papers and office litter, and three dirty coffee mugs sat beside the keyboard.

Jonty shut the door behind them and produced a couple of bottles of water from a small fridge in the corner.

'You must be parched,' he said, taking his seat behind the desk, 'the humidity's the killer here, y'know.'

'Cheers.' Archer cracked his bottle and took a sip. 'So, you've obviously been briefed to expect us?'

'That's right.' Jonty nodded enthusiastically. 'Not much happens here, y'know, so it's always nice to have visitors. It's usually just the usual boring bits and pieces, y'know, maybe a bit of smuggling and whatnot. Bit boring, really.' He laughed suddenly, a short, nervous laugh as if he suddenly realised he'd said too much. 'Don't repeat that, of course, I was just joking, y'know.'

'Of course.' Archer smiled, taking a liking to this little guy. 'We should be here no more than a couple of days, all going well.'

'Great, great.' Jonty nodded enthusiastically again. 'How about dinner then? There's a great little place round by the wharf, fantastic crayfish, y'know?'

Archer felt Tracy's eyes on him. 'Love to mate,' he said easily, 'but it's probably not the best idea, given we're not really here and everyone will know who you are.'

Jonty's smile faltered, and Tracy stepped in to save him.

'We don't want to compromise you,' she told him with a solemn look, 'it's more important that you can stay detached from us while we're here.'

Jonty nodded and seemed to perk up slightly as he saw the sense of what she'd said. 'Too true,' he agreed, 'don't mind me getting ahead of myself.'

'But if you're ever back in Auckland...' Tracy smiled, and Archer saw the small man brighten again, making the natural assumption that Tracy would be there.

'Of course, of course. Haven't been back in a while...'

'So,' Archer interrupted, keen to get back to the point, 'if we need you we'll give you a bell. I've got your mobile number. We're down at Aggie's, and we'll let you know when we leave.'

'Great, great stuff, y'know.'

'In the meantime,' Archer continued, his tone turning serious, 'we need access to the black box.'

Jonty paused as he absorbed this, then nodded again. Archer figured he had probably never had this request before. He knew they were there to follow up a lead on the yacht owner who could potentially lead them to Yassar; he probably hadn't realised how far that may need to go.

Jonty nodded again and went to an in-built cupboard behind his desk, set into an internal wall. He unlocked it with a key, opened the door, and crouched to access a large safe on the floor. Once it was open he stepped back again and gestured towards it with one hand, inviting them in.

'It's probably a bit light but it's all yours,' he said gravely, 'take your time, y'know. I'll just go and get a coffee.'

He scooped up his three dirty mugs and left the office, closing the door again behind them.

Archer went to the safe and surveyed the contents. Every embassy around the world had a black box, which was over and above the armaments they held as a matter of course for self defence. The black box contained a number of items of use to agents, which were intended to be untraceable. It was a way around having to rely on the diplomatic pouches in the case of emergency.

This one was sorely lacking. It constituted a small amount of electronic gear, which he ignored, infrared binoculars, a couple of pistol cases, a box of demolitions gear, a box of ammunition, and a rifle broken down into a padded case.

He removed the pistol cases and checked them. Matching Beretta 92Fs, civilian versions of the standard US military-issue sidearm. 9mm with a 15-round magazine. He took the guns and the spare magazines, and put the cases back in the safe.

The rifle case opened to show an Armalite AR-7, a 7-shot semi-automatic .22 which Archer had used before. It was lightweight and reliable, the moving parts could be stowed in the butt stock, and it even floated. It had a 9x scope with it and a suppressor, plus a couple of spare magazines. He took the weapon and replaced the case, then checked the ammo case.

Two boxes of 9mm for the pistols and a single box of sub-sonic

.22 rounds were added to the pile. Two black nylon Safariland holsters were joined by the infrared binos, then Archer closed the safe and spun the dial. Tracy offered no input into the selections; munitions were his department. She couldn't miss his scowl, however.

She opened his daypack instead and held it while he loaded the equipment into it. They had just finished when Jonty returned, knocking first and announcing himself. Archer smiled to himself – the man had an air of pronounced "spyishness" about him.

'Well, all done?' he asked, putting his coffee mug down on his desk.

'For what it is,' Archer replied shortly. 'I've got better supplies at home.'

Jonty flushed with the criticism but said nothing.

Archer shouldered the day pack. 'We'll be in touch within a couple of days and give you an update of some sort.' He extended his hand. 'Thanks for your help, Jonty.'

They shook then Tracy did likewise, before Jonty escorted them back out to Reception.

'Good to see you guys,' he said loudly, for the benefit of the receptionist, 'take care, y'know.'

'Cheers mate.'

They left the High Commission and walked back towards the hotel.

'He's an excitable little chap,' Tracy commented, a touch sarcastically Archer thought.

'He is,' he agreed, 'but sincere. I get the feeling he's the sort we could rely on if needed.'

Tracy didn't reply and he took this to indicate disagreement. He was getting a little bit sick of the condescending attitude, but bit his tongue. It wasn't worth arguing about. The pitiful state of the black box didn't help. Typical NZ approach; number eight wire all over.

They reached the hotel and ordered lunch at the lobby cafe on the way through to their room, promising to be back shortly.

Once in their room, Archer went to the bedroom and closed the curtains. He opened the bag and tossed Tracy a pistol. She caught it with ease and looked at him questioningly.

'This is yours,' he told her brusquely, 'get to know it and after lunch we'll strip them down.'

He put a box of ammo and two magazines with one of the holsters on the table in front of her.

'We'll load the magazines now so we're ready, then have lunch.'

Just then they both heard a chirping coming from Tracy's bag. She quickly dug out a cell phone Archer hadn't seen before and answered cheerfully. He saw her brow furrow into a frown.

'Hello....hello, Ruth? It's Emma, you called me?'

Archer had a feeling of impending doom in his gut and the expression on Tracy's face told him she felt it too. She stared at the phone for a moment then tossed it on the bed.

'That's strange...that was Ruth's CHIS phone. There was someone there but they didn't say anything.'

'Has it happened before?'

Tracy looked at him, perplexed. 'Never.' She grabbed her normal cell phone and dialled a number from memory.

In less than a minute she had relayed her concern to a colleague and requested a welfare check on the informer. She put the phone away and came back to the table. She saw him glance at her second phone with a raised eyebrow.

'Handler phone,' she said simply. 'Only used for sources.'

Archer nodded and picked up a magazine.

They worked in silence, each thumbing rounds into their own magazines before loading the weapons, holstering them, and stashing them behind the fridge. Archer watched her work, and noted she appeared comfortable with the gun.

He left the Armalite disassembled and stashed it with its ammo under the seat of the sofa. They cleaned their hands to remove the smell of gun oil, and returned to the cafe to find their lunch waiting for them. It was simple chicken stir fry with noodles, heavy on the oil, and they ate it in cane chairs, flicking through magazines in silence.

Archer went to the counter to order another drink, and as he did so he heard Tracy's mobile buzz behind him with an incoming text. He turned and watched her face fall as she read it. She looked up as he sat back down, giving her a questioning look.

'Bad news?' he asked.

She nodded slowly. 'Boyle's escaped.'

Archer's brow creased. 'Casualties?'

'Two contractors dead. Matthew managed to escape but obviously couldn't stop him.' Tracy let out her breath slowly and put the phone away.

'When?'

'About four hours ago.'

Archer nodded. 'Not good.'

Tracy opened her mouth to speak but was cut off by the ringing of her phone. She answered abruptly and listened. As Archer watched her, her face went white. She put a hand to her forehead, distress written all over her face. He knew what she was going to say before she disconnected the call.

'How?' he asked. 'And when?'

'Drugs,' Tracy whispered, her face ashen. 'She was found on her lounge floor with a needle hanging out her arm. The landlady rang the cops because her door was wide open.'

'Your man?' He didn't want to use names out loud, so used the Irish slang instead.

Tracy pulled face. 'Who knows. Early indication from the cops is it was likely to have been an accidental OD.'

'Reasonable assumption, except for the recent events.'

'The cops were there when the Special Branch guy did a drive-by. He rang straight back once he knew what was going on.'

'They know how long ago it happened?'

'Didn't say.' Tracy shook her head in bewilderment. 'I know what you're thinking. I may've been the last person she called.'

'Well,' Archer muttered, 'that just changed things slightly.'

36

The rest of the afternoon was spent killing time.
Archer caught up with the news – the main story in the UK being the big shootout in Cornwall between two opposing gangs. A number of guns had been recovered and one gangster was in Police custody for interrogation.

There was no mention of the crashed helicopter and enquiries were continuing. Archer had to give it to the spooks, they'd done a great job of keeping a lid on it so far.

Tracy got a couple of updates but nothing of any consequence until near dinner time, when her base called to let her know that a man had been seen leaving Ruth's flat an hour or so before the landlady called the Police.

The description roughly matched Boyle, but could also have been half the rest of the local male population. The Special Branch detective had confirmed that Ruth's burn phone was missing from the address. They were trying to track it but without luck so far. They knew that the phone had been used to call Tracy but that seemed to be the only activity on it in the last day or so.

They eventually went for dinner at the place Jonty had

mentioned, and ate in near silence. Archer tried a couple of weak jokes to snap Tracy out of her slump, and failed miserably. He gave up and ordered dessert coffees instead.

There was little news the next day and Tracy was getting agitated at the lack of updates. She finally rang Livingstone and her manner verged on being brusque as she demanded an update. She listened for a couple of minutes before disconnecting. Archer could see the tension ease slightly in her face as she put the phone down.

'They haven't made any real progress,' she explained, 'but it's looking more and more like just an overdose. She was still on the gear, and she'd OD'd once before, a couple of years ago.'

'What about the guy seen leaving?' Archer enquired.

'Haven't tracked him down yet. It was probably a dealer, or a client.'

'Or Boyle.'

'Yeah, maybe....the timing doesn't really work though.'

'Why not?'

'Well, Matthew spoke to her about two hours before the landlady found her, so about an hour before this guy was apparently seen leaving. He said she was fine then.'

Archer frowned. 'How does that affect the timing though, if he rang her? How does he know what was going on at her place from the other end of the phone?' He sounded irritated and Tracy looked at him sharply. 'I know you all think he's a goddamn genius, but can he see through walls now too?'

It was her turn to scowl now. 'He went to see her, okay? In person. And everything was fine.'

'How does that mean Boyle didn't come along afterwards and knock her off?' he pressed.

Tracy's lips pursed and he knew the argument was going nowhere.

'Matthew is pretty well known to the Provos, okay? Part of the reason he moved to Six was his face got known over the water. If Boyle was lurking around, scoping the place out, he would've seen Matthew and he wouldn't have gone near the place.'

He opened his mouth to reply and she held up a hand.

'Just drop it, alright? It's in hand.'

Archer shook his head in frustration and grabbed his towel, muttering that he was going for a swim.

37

The villa was clearly illuminated through the infrared lenses of the Bushnell binoculars. Archer took his time, methodically scanning the property section by section. What he saw was not good.

He slid back carefully into the slight depression where Tracy lay waiting, covering their rear. He leaned close to her head, close enough to smell her. Her hair brushed his face as he whispered.

'There's an outside cordon of infrared beams, all the way around, about thirty metres in front of us. There are at least two tree-mounted cameras that I could see on this side, probably motion-activated. There's a guard roaming the inner cordon, carrying a Winchester semi auto shotgun. There's at least one guard inside the house, couldn't see what he had but a long of some sort.'

Tracy nodded her understanding.

'No sign of the target.'

She nodded again. 'So; plan?'

Archer cocked his head. 'Well, we can beat the infrared cordon, I can take out the external guard, we can probably deal with whoever's inside, but those cameras are a problem. If we had enough time and some sheets of polystyrene, I could beat them too.' He scanned the trees with the binos again. 'Problem is, I don't know how many or where they are, and if we miss one it doesn't matter if we beat everything else; we'd be walking straight into an ambush.'

'I thought SAS stood for Speed, Aggression, Surprise,' Tracy jibed him.

'It does,' he agreed, 'but not Stupid And Sloppy. If you fancy making a run for the front door from here be my guest; I'll cover the rear and send a nice card to your parents.' He frowned. 'Let's bug out and come up with a better plan.'

Tracy moved wordlessly ahead of him in a commando crawl through the undergrowth, her boots mere inches from his face. The night was heavy and humid, the buzz of insects loud.

He cradled the suppressed AR-7 in his arms and kept his head on a swivel, constantly scanning, checking, pausing to listen as they headed back towards the Jeep they'd stashed off the side of the mountain road.

Suddenly he heard something and paused, his left hand snaking out to grab Tracy's ankle. Silence. No birdsong. No buzz of insects. Archer's eyes probed the darkness and he carefully pulled the binos from under his shirt.

As soon as he raised them he saw the threat. Two large Samoans approaching from the right, straight towards them. The one in the front had a set of night vision goggles strapped to his face and was locked on the two crawling intruders just twenty metres away. The one behind him had no goggles but carried a shotgun at the ready.

The front man opened his mouth to shout and Archer rolled on his side, bringing the AR-7 up and snapping a quick shot at them.

Tracy raised herself and bolted at the same time, drawing her Beretta and doubling over as she ran, one hand in front to protect her face from low branches.

The lead enemy ducked and scrabbled for a holstered pistol. The shotgunner stepped around him and brought his barrel to bear. Archer triggered a double tap, the little rifle barely twitching in his hands as he dropped the lead man.

A shotgun blast ripped the night air and birds screeched above him as buckshot shredded the leaves and branches. Archer rolled again, scrabbled forward a couple of metres and took a knee, coming into the aim again. The shotgunner let rip again, firing blind and wide, the muzzle blast exposing him badly in the pitch darkness.

Archer popped off another double tap, knew he'd missed and ran. Branches slapped at him as he crashed through the undergrowth, and he heard another shotgun blast behind him. He ignored it and ran on, knowing that, unless his enemy was highly trained and lucky, he would be hard pressed to nail a running man in the thick vegetation.

He reached the road and turned, dropping to a knee again, the AR-7 coming up as the shotgunner crashed towards him with the grace of a drunk hippo. Archer emptied his last two shots at him, saw the man drop, and bolted again. Headlights were coming up behind him from the direction of the villa's driveway and he heard the throaty roar of an engine being worked hard.

Ahead another set of lights came on in the undergrowth, bouncing as the Jeep was manoeuvred out onto the road. He changed magazines as he ran, chambering a new round. He felt wildly inadequate with just a .22 in his hands, and for the hundredth time that day he mentally cursed the poor capabilities of the embassy's black box.

Tracy was revving the engine as he reached the Jeep and yanked the driver's door open. She scrambled across to the passenger's seat and grabbed the Armalite from him as he jumped in.

The Jeep leaped forward as Archer mashed the accelerator down and the tyres screeched and grabbed at the seal. Headlights approached fast from behind them. Archer chopped up through the gears, riding the gas and clutch, fighting the wheel as the Jeep tried to swerve off into the darkness.

A shotgun blasted loudly behind them and they heard bird shot pinging off the rear panels. The headlights got brighter behind them, the full beams lighting up the inside of the Jeep as a ute closed in. More shots sounded over the roar of the Jeep's engine and Tracy ducked. The fabric canopy twitched as a couple of shots got close to the mark.

'Keep them at bay,' Archer shouted, down changing to enter a corner, goosing the gas to keep the revs up.

Tracy turned in her seat and brought the AR-7 up to the shoulder, kneeling as she tried to get a bead on their attackers.

Another couple of shots thudded into the back of the Jeep, and Archer's wing mirror exploded in a shower of glass and plastic.

Tracy squeezed off a quick volley of shots, causing the attackers' ute to falter for a second before accelerating hard again to bear down on them.

They hit a straight and Archer floored it, the Jeep responding but he knew it was not enough.

'Cut loose at them,' he shouted, 'we can't outrun them in this.'

Tracy responded by emptying the magazine before snatching out her Beretta and stabbing it forward. She only had time to unleash one shot before the gunman in the ute emptied his own magazine into the Jeep. The windscreen spider webbed with multiple impacts and the headrest beneath Tracy's left elbow blew apart in a cloud of stuffing. She yelped and grabbed for a hand hold, yelling a warning as she saw the ute suddenly charge them.

The Jeep lurched forward and rocked dangerously, metal screeching and plastic shattering as the ute rammed it from behind.

Archer swore angrily and grappled with the wheel, almost getting it straight again before the second thud threw them forward again. The Jeep swerved, the left wheels hit loose gravel and the tail flicked out. He steered into the skid, chopping the gear stick into neutral and checking both sides.

The Jeep was still coming back in line when the ute rammed them for the third time, and Archer knew this was it. The Jeep spun and the wheel was ripped from his hands. Tracy was thrown first against the side window then crashed into Archer, her skull slamming against his shoulder hard enough to instantly deaden it.

Undergrowth rushed at them and all they could hear was the roar of engines and screaming of tortured tyres. Archer grabbed hold of

Tracy with one hand and threw the other over his head as he ducked down, bracing for the impact.

A hefty tree trunk leaped out of the darkness and slammed into the Jeep, spinning it again and throwing it off balance. The Jeep rocked onto two wheels, wobbled, then dropped onto its right side and slid.

A tree branch crashed through the driver's side window and glass burst over them and the Jeep stopped with a thud. Archer's seatbelt jerked tight at his waist and across his chest, cutting off his air and dangling him sideways like a rag doll, Tracy dropping him his grasp as he fumbled weakly with the seatbelt.

His fingers felt like catcher's gloves and his vision was blurring with the lack of oxygen. If he could just get the buckle undone…

Through the fog in his head Archer heard voices and then the crashing of feet in the undergrowth around the wrecked Jeep. He fumbled for the Beretta but it had been jarred loose in the crash, and before he could find it hands reached through the smashed window and grabbed him. He felt himself dragged out and dumped on the ground, then a boot slammed into his ribs.

He arched in pain and took another one to the gut. He rolled over and saw a burly Samoan hauling Tracy out of the windscreen. He tossed her to the ground like a rag doll and she groaned. Archer wanted to reach out and console her but his tongue felt thick and he couldn't focus enough to string a sentence together.

Another boot hit him in the back and he let out a groan, but it was just the start. A hail of kicks and punches rained down on him and he curled himself into a ball to protect his vital organs as laughter sounded from those around him.

Eventually the assault eased and he slowly uncurled himself and rolled onto his back. A sweaty, smiling Samoan face peered down at him, and a machete glinted in the headlights.

'You made bad move, you honky shit,' the man grinned evilly.

He lowered the blade to Archer's throat and pressed it firmly against the skin. Archer held perfectly still, knowing his life was in this thug's hands.

'I get my chance.'

The man stood, sheathed the machete, and grabbed Archer by the arm. He hauled him up and pushed him against the side of the wrecked Jeep. Archer tried to catch his breath and glanced about, sizing up his chances.

Another man, very tall, was tying Tracy's hands behind her back, and a second, short and stocky, stood to the side with a revolver hanging at his side. Archer subconsciously clocked it as a decades-old Smith and Wesson Model 10, a .38 Special with wooden grips. Notoriously inaccurate, but at four metres it was just as likely to blow a hole in his head as a cannon.

'Hey, no looking!'

His captor, who he mentally logged as the middle-sized man, spun Archer around to face him, and smashed a knee into his crotch. Blinding pain rocked through him and he collapsed forward, clutching at his crotch and gasping for air.

Strong hands wrestled his arms behind his back and tied them tightly, then he was dragged to his feet and hustled past the wreck to the thugs' ute. The men lifted him over the tailgate and dumped him on his face. A few seconds later Tracy was dumped on top of him and he found himself face to face with her. Blood leaked down her forehead from a shallow cut and her face was sweaty and dirty.

'Okay?' he murmured stupidly.

Tracy's lips twitched into something resembling a smile. 'Great. Good driving.'

Archer tried to smile. 'Thanks.'

'You, shut up.'

A fist slammed into his kidney from behind and fresh pain enveloped him. They fell silent while the ute started up and moved off. The tall man climbed into the back and sat over them, his attention caught by Tracy. He leaned forward and ran a long finger down her cheek. She flinched away with a scowl.

The man chuckled to himself, deep and throaty, and removed his hand. But Archer noted that he never shifted his gaze from her body.

Things were not looking up.

38

After a few minutes on the main road they turned off onto a bumpy track and headed into the bush, before pulling up in a dirt clearing. The men climbed out and roughly dragged their captives over the tailboard of the ute.

Archer saw they were outside a dilapidated shack the size of a single garage, surrounded by bush.

They were dragged forward by the three big men into the shack, and shoved into armless wooden chairs facing each other across the room. Coarse twine was produced and they were tied to the chairs by their arms, with their wrists still bound behind them. The room had a dirty wooden floor, a couple of windows with closed shutters and was sparsely furnished. A hurricane lamp burned on the table against a wall, and a pot-belly stove was throwing heat into the room.

The shorter man then took the time to administer a thump to the side of Archer's head which knocked him to the floor with his head ringing and stars in his eyes. The men guffawed at the act of brutality before hauling him back upright and allowing the short man to repeat the performance.

Archer went with the flow, letting them have their fun for now and all the while planning their escape. Things looked pretty bleak from where he was sitting. They were miles from any help, caged with three thugs who seemed to get off on violence, and they were securely tied up.

He lay there and caught his breath, watching the men. The middle-sized man removed the machete from his belt and leaned it by the door. Archer figured it was about three metres away from him. As the man turned, Archer noted he also wore a diving knife sheathed on his belt. Watching these animals and listening to their pseudo-gangster talk made him hate them with a passion. He determined that if he got even the slightest of chances, he would happily kill any or all of them.

Looking over at Tracy as he was picked up again, he could see the terror in her eyes. The middle-sized man turned to her and with a lecherous leer, and in one quick swipe he ripped the front of her shirt open all the way to her waist. He grabbed first one breast then the other, pawing roughly and making her squeal with pain.

The taller man stepped over and shouldered his mate aside before ripping her bra open and exposing her to their gaze.

Archer could see the lust in their faces as all three turned their attention to her now, groping at her and grunting like animals.

He stared hard at her across the gap, willing her to be strong. Tears rolled from her eyes, whether from pain or fear he couldn't tell. She met his gaze and held it, taking a shuddering breath before pulling her head back and unleashing a gob of spit into the face of the taller man.

He recoiled back then lashed out and back-handed her viciously across the mouth, knocking her chair against the wall. The short man caught her by the arm and pulled her upright. The tall man hooked her in the temple now, throwing her to the side again where the middle man caught her and righted the chair.

A trickle of blood ran from Tracy's mouth as she looked up at the tall man and bared her teeth at him.

'Fuck you,' she whispered.

'Ha ha.' The tall man hefted his crotch at her with a grin. 'I think I fuck you.'

Archer could see this spiralling out of control very quickly, and interjected with a shouted 'Hey!'

The short man turned and drove a fist into his gut, winding him, then grabbed him by the hair and pulled his head back. Nose to nose, the Samoan leered at him. His breath was putrid with fish and beer.

'No one can hear yo scream, bro,' he chuckled, 'but I still rip yo tongue out yo head.'

Archer eyeballed him and sucked air in through his nose.

'You touch her again, you filthy fuckin' animal,' he hissed, 'and I'll kill you.' He tossed a glance at the other two men, who had stopped now and were listening. 'And your little boyfriends.'

The short man flushed with anger and straightened up, cracking the knuckles of his right hand and shaking it out before setting his feet in a boxing stance.

'Yo got a big mouf, bro.'

The right jab came straight at Archer's face and he managed to pull his head left and just catch it on the cheekbone, but it was still hard enough to rock him back in the chair.

He looked at the man with a scornful sneer. 'Pussy. You hit like a fa'afafine.'

The other two men chuckled at his reference to the transvestites, and anger twisted the short man's face. His left shot out and smashed into Archer's jaw, followed by a right-left-right combo which tossed him around like a cork on the tide, the room swaying before him as he rolled with each punch.

The short man stepped back and prepared himself for the next round, and Archer caught Tracy's eye.

'Thank you,' she mouthed to him, knowing that while the men were focussed on him, they were leaving her alone.

A car engine sounded outside followed by doors slamming and the crunch of footsteps approaching. The door opened and a pair of newcomers stepped inside, banging the door closed behind them.

'Well well lads,' Boyle said with a cheery grin, looking at each of them in turn, 'what do we have here then?'

Beside him, Yassar leered at Tracy. Archer's heart sank as he realised their predicament had just got worse.

The Irishman paused to glance at their passports then stepped into the space between the two captives and rubbed his hands together as he ran an appraising eye over them.

'I trust my friends have been treating you well?' he inquired, nodding as if to confirm it to himself. He paused as he took in Tracy's nakedness. 'And hello to you, Ms Spencer. So this is what all the men at the firm have been missing all this time, eh?' He glanced over at Archer. 'Unless you've had a piece of this, Kiwi? No, I didn't think so.' He grinned at the three Samoans beside him. 'She likes the ladies, y'know lads.'

The tall man hefted his crotch again with a leer. 'Maybe she like the black snake, boss,' he grinned.

Boyle nodded. 'You'll get yer chance, Afa,' he said, 'although ye may need to get in line behind my Saudi friend here. But first, I need to have a little chat with our very special agent.'

He knelt down in front of Tracy, who eyed him with contempt. He patted her knee affectionately. Yassar moved over to stand behind him, his eyes fixated on Tracy's breasts.

'It's a shame it all came to this, Tracy, it really is. But it was your choice.' Boyle shrugged as if his hands were tied. 'There are always consequences to actions, and I think we're all going to learn a little lesson about that tonight.'

He stood again and took his jacket off. 'I don't have a lot of time, so let's get straight to the point.' He stood in front of her now, his back to Archer. 'Who got wee Ruthie to sell me out to the spooks?'

'I don't know.' Tracy's voice had a quiver in it as she spoke.

'I don't believe you.' Boyle's own voice was strong and deep. 'I've lost many people dear to me over the years, and I've lived with a target on my back since I was a kid. You pricks were supposed to leave me alone; that was what the Good Friday Agreement was all about.'

'It was a get-out-of-jail card,' she replied bravely, 'not a license to run guns.'

Boyle paused to study her face carefully. 'Ye may think ye can outlast me, sweetheart, but I promise ye won't. Nobody ever has.'

'You fancy yourself, don't you?' Archer interjected.

Boyle didn't look at him, just tossed his head at Afa. The tall man stepped in and delivered a booming roundhouse to Archer's head which bounced off the wall behind him. Thunder flashes went off in his skull.

'Let me get the ball rolling then. I know wee Ruthie got turned,' Boyle continued. 'I found her burn phone, which led me to ye.' His eyes glinted. 'That were me that rung ye, so don't try and deny it. I recognise yer voice.'

Archer felt his heart sink further.

'But what I don't understand is why she was in the way. Why she was killed.'

'Well it wasn't us,' Tracy retorted hotly. 'Maybe you need to look closer to home.'

'I don't have a home, thanks to youse traitorous bastards,' Boyle spat. 'Everything I had is gone.'

'Lie down with dogs, mate, you wake up with fleas.'

Archer had to admire the conviction in Tracy's voice now, at the same time as he knew it would do no good. Boyle was going to kill her tonight and everybody in the room knew it.

'Aye, that's right.' Boyle leaned down into her face, dropping his voice to a venomous whisper. 'And you're the biggest bitch of all.'

He placed his hand round her throat and squeezed, cutting off her air. Tracy braced up, still eyeballing him as he applied more pressure.

'I oughta kill you right now,' he whispered. 'Just snap your neck and get it over with. But you hurt me, Tracy. So I think it's only fair that I cause you some pain in return.'

He straightened again and let go of her throat. Tracy gulped down air and watched him as he went to his jacket on the table. The room went silent as Boyle removed two tools from his jacket pocket. One was a pair of pliers, the other a set of wire cutters.

He turned to Tracy again and smiled as he held the tools up for her to see. 'And let the games begin,' he purred.

Tracy bucked in her chair at the same time as Archer pushed away from the wall. The tall man grabbed her by the shoulder and held her down, while the other two thugs grabbed Archer and pushed him back.

'You gutless fuckin' maggot,' Archer snarled helplessly, 'you like hurting girls do ya? Fuckin' big man.'

Boyle cast an eye at him then to the men holding him. 'Shut him up,' he ordered.

The shorter man grinned and cracked his knuckles again. Archer had just a split-second to tense up before the fist drove into his gut, but wasn't prepared for the middle man's crack across the jaw. He sagged and blinked to clear his vision, powerless to resist as a dirty rag was jammed into his mouth. It tasted of paraffin and made him gag, but was made worse when the middle man tied it in place with a piece of cloth and knotted it tightly around his head.

'I'd suggest ye don't let it go past this point,' Boyle advised Tracy, sounding like a parent talking to a naughty child. 'Three strikes and ye're out. So let's start at the lower end of the scale.'

The tall man lifted her, chair and all, and carried her to the table. Archer sat helplessly just a metre away. He watched with dread as the tall man untied Tracy's right hand and moved it towards the table. She tried to scratch at his face but he caught her hand easily and pushed it flat on the table top.

Boyle pulled a chair over and sat beside her. He placed the pliers and wire cutters on the table beside him.

'Who turned Ruthie to sell me out?' Boyle said, watching her carefully.

'I don't know,' Tracy told him forcefully.

Boyle shook his head and tut-tutted softly.

He took hold of her hand and she instinctively closed it into a fist. The tall man leaned over and effortlessly pried her hand open, holding her fingers straight.

'Thank you, Afa.'

Boyle took hold of the little finger and in one quick motion, he popped the joint.

Tracy's scream ripped through Archer's heart and he bucked against the hands holding him. Tracy's face was screwed up and tears rolled down her cheeks. Her finger poked out to the side at a sickening angle.

'Now, again.' Boyle continued, as if nothing had happened. 'Tell me who.'

His hand rested on Tracy's, fingers on the next digit now.

Tracy shook her head hard, her face still screwed in pain. She sucked in a breath and forced her eyes open.

'I don't fuckin' know!'

Boyle's hand moved again and she shrieked as her ring finger popped in his grip.

She screamed again, long and piercing. Archer felt sick to his stomach and he couldn't take his eyes off the Irish terrorist. The man's expression had barely changed. There was neither pleasure nor distaste; it was merely a task that needed to be completed.

Archer's bellows of rage were muffled by the gag and he knew there was nothing he could do to stop this brutality. He slumped back in his chair and tried to catch his breath. The bindings were tight around his wrists and waist; he had barely an inch of slack in which to move. It didn't seem likely that he would be able to break free of them any time soon. He had no weapons to hand and nothing with which to cut the ropes.

As hopeless situations went, this was pretty up there as far as he could see.

Archer felt his heart rate slowing and forced himself to focus. Nothing was ever hopeless; he just had to find his way out.

Boyle slapped Tracy on the leg to get her attention. She slowly turned her head to look at him. Blood trickled from her mouth and tears stained her cheeks. Her eyes were still defiant.

'Ye've got some spunk, girl, I'll give ye that.' He nodded with admiration. 'But it won't do no good. Everybody talks.'

He leaned closer to her, looking directly into her eyes. 'Everybody.'

Archer ignored the talking and scanned the room, looking for anything he could possibly use, given the chance. He rolled his shoulders as he did so, testing the grip of the two thugs. There was a bit of slack there as they were distracted by watching the main event. He flexed his fingers again to test the bindings for the hundredth time, and as he did so, his fingernail tapped against something hard. Something slightly protruding from the seat of the chair; a nail?

He felt for it again. Maybe not a nail, but whatever it was it was something, and it gave him hope.

Boyle stood and went to the pot-belly stove. He took a steel poker from the kindling bucket beside it and jabbed it into the heart of the fire. He returned to his seat and drummed his fingers on the table, fixing Tracy with his gaze again.

'Come on Tracy,' he urged, 'cut to the chase eh? Spill and it'll all be over.'

'You,' she grated, 'can go to hell.'

'Aye,' he acknowledged, 'I probably will. But I'm not the only one.'

He returned to the fire and came back with the poker. The tip of it glowed red hot now. Every eye in the room was on him as he sat back down and held the poker up in front of his captive.

'Feel like talking?' he asked.

Tracy snarled at him again, and in one quick movement, Boyle leaned past her and stabbed the poker into Archer's chest.

Archer bucked in agony as the heat seared through his shirt and pierced the skin, feeling like it drove straight through the core of him. The stench of burning flesh and hair filled his nostrils and he gagged involuntarily. The pain was so intense he wanted to pass out to make it end.

Boyle withdrew the steel and appraised him.

'He's a tough cookie, yer boy,' he conceded to Tracy. 'I wonder how long he'll last before I break him?' He smiled mirthlessly. 'Or before I break you?'

Blinding pain seared through Archer's soul and he wanted to die.

He squeezed his eyes tightly and tried to ignore the pain. He forced himself to focus on the task at hand, catching the wrist bindings on the head of the nail and pulling at it.

Boyle returned the poker to the fire and sat again. He picked up the pliers and showed them to his captive.

'I'll give ye ten seconds to tell me the truth,' he told her, 'otherwise I'll start me dental work. Ten.'

Tracy tried to stay calm, but he could see the fear in her eyes.

'Five.'

Archer tried to catch her eye but she stubbornly avoided him.

'One.'

Boyle stood and reached for her. The tall man took hold of her jaw in one giant paw and arched her head back. Boyle seized hold of her throat and throttled her until she gasped and opened her mouth. He reached in with the pliers and gripped a molar at the back of her jaw. Tracy's scream was muffled by the tool.

'Last chance,' Boyle told her. 'No?'

He gripped hard and wrenched the tooth from the gum. Tracy wailed like a newborn and strained against the hands holding her.

Boyle held the bloodied tooth up to her face and waited for her to stop screaming. Gradually her cries slowed to chest-heaving sobs. Blood flowed down her chin onto the front of her shirt.

'Who was it?' He leaned down into her face, staring intently into her eyes. 'And who killed her?'

Archer willed her to keep her mouth shut. He could feel the strands of the rope giving way slowly as he worked it against the nail head, but he needed more time.

Tracy's voice was barely audible. Boyle leaned closer to listen.

'Speak up, Ms Spencer,' he told her. 'I need the name.'

She lifted her head and looked at him through her tears. 'Livingstone,' she rasped. 'I took her over from him.'

Boyle nodded slowly, his face finally showing a flicker of excitement. He stood and rubbed his hands together. 'The famous Mr Matthew Livingstone. Now that weren't so hard now, were it?' He tossed his head to the tall man holding her. 'She's all yours, big man.'

He checked his watch and glanced at Yassar. 'We've got a plane to catch. God, I hate London in the winter.'

'What about him, boss?'

The tall man indicated towards Archer, who appeared to have gone into a dazed state.

Boyle shrugged dismissively. 'Whatever. Kill him.'

The Irishman turned and headed to the door, where Yassar was waiting. He paused there and glanced back to Tracy.

'All the best, spy lady. It's been a hell of a ride.' He grinned coldly. 'Oh, one more thing.' He drew a compact Seecamp .32 auto from beneath his shirt and hefted it in his palm. 'Lovely weapon,' he commented.

He turned again and pointed the weapon at Yassar. The Saudi's eyes bulged and he started to raise his hands.

'Sorry pal, business is business.' Boyle triggered a double tap and blew Yassar's brains across the wall behind him. The body dropped with a thud and Boyle gave it another double tap to be sure.

Gun smoke hung in the still air.

'Whoever said blood was thicker than water obviously never met the Saudis,' he noted. With that he was gone, and a few seconds later the engine started up again and moved away.

39

The three Samoans looked at each other and an understanding passed between them.

Afa dragged Tracy backwards on her chair to the other wall, facing Archer again. He looked at the white guy and figured he was out of the game. Bloodied and battered and staring dazedly at the floor.

He gave the shorter man, Hosea, a flick of the head and turned back to Tracy. Solomon, the middle-sized man, stayed beside the slumped form of Archer. He fingered the diving knife on his belt and waited impatiently for his turn.

Afa slapped Tracy's cheek, hard enough to shock her into focus, and she stared at him with terrified eyes.

'So you don' like boys, huh miss?' His teeth gleamed white in the flickering light. 'We see 'bout dat, huh?'

He started to undo his pants, and Hosea chuckled as he watched.

'Heh heh heh, do it boy, do dat!'

Tracy spat at him and saw the gob slide down Afa's chest. He cocked his fist and smashed it into her face, snapping her head sideways. Her left eyebrow split and blood cascaded over the eye and down her cheek.

Just as Afa began to drop his pants, Archer made his move. The last strand of binding round his wrists broke and he shrugged his arms free of the rope round them. Solomon felt the movement and looked down, a second too late to stop Archer from snatching the knife from his belt.

Solomon grabbed for him as Archer leaped to his feet and thrust the diving knife up in a short jab. The blade pierced the thug's side below the ribs and drove upwards before Archer yanked it free and shoved him aside. Hosea reacted quickly and came for him, hands out defensively, body position low and wide like a wrestler. He obviously fancied himself with his hands, and thankfully focussed on that rather than drawing his gun. If he'd been smarter, the fight would have ended a lot sooner.

Archer shifted the knife into a better grip and moved to gain space. The chair was still hanging off his waist by the rope and hitting the back of his legs as he moved. He ignored it and concentrated on the threats around him.

Afa scrabbled at his pants and tried to turn. As he did so, Tracy drove up and crashed into his side with her shoulder, making him stagger off balance. He threw a fist at her but missed, and Tracy continued to drive with her legs, shoving him across the room and into the wall where Archer had sat just moments before.

Archer dodged around them and Hosea made his move, rushing forward and going for a combination of jabs at Archer's face.

The stocky Samoan was more agile than he looked, and he managed to land a glancing blow to Archer's jaw before the knife swiped across his forearm and opened it up. He pulled back and clasped a hand to the wound, snarling like a dog.

Afa slapped at the woman pushing against him, turning and trying to grab her. Tracy's skull came up and cracked him under the jaw, snapping his mouth shut and causing his teeth to chomp into his tongue hard enough to draw blood.

Archer feinted with a right stab and gave Hosea a left cross to the jaw, not a vintage shot but it kept him at bay.

Afa's knees buckled beneath him and he went down. Tracy's knee smashed into his nose as he slumped to his knees and a fan of blood sprayed out. He fell backwards against the wall and she drove a heel into his face, then again.

Archer hacked through the twine and dropped the chair, but as he stepped away from it Hosea rushed him again. Archer twisted and slashed at him, managing to grab his shirt as they both went down.

Tracy screamed and slammed her heel into Afa's face again, hearing bone crunch beneath her foot.

Archer wrestled with Hosea as they rolled on the floor, snapping his head forward in repeated attempts to butt him, and scrabbling at his face with his free hand. He got his fingers into Hosea's right eye and dug in, gouging and scratching. The thug screeched and butted him in the forehead with a head as hard as concrete.

Lights exploded in Archer's eyes and the back of his head slammed into the floor with a thud. Hosea took advantage of the moment to back off and wind up his fist.

Afa flopped sideways to the floor, unconscious. Blood flowed freely from his smashed nose and lips. Tracy drew her foot back and toe-hacked him directly to the Adam's apple.

Archer saw the fist coming and half-rolled to the side, letting Hosea's punch sail past and hit the floor. He shoved and got his knees up far enough to heave the thug off him. Hosea caught his balance on his haunches and came again, throwing himself forward in an attempt to pin Archer beneath him.

Archer rolled again, kicking free of the ropes and the chair before scrambling to his feet. He spun and delivered a punt to Hosea's face. The thug fell back, clutching at his bloodied face. His knees were splayed and Archer gave him a second kick, this time to the testicles.

Tracy cocked her foot and drove it down into Afa's throat again. A murderous rage had descended over her and she was functioning on auto-pilot.

Hosea folded at the waist and pulled his knees up. He rolled onto his side and vomited on the floor. Archer stood over him and sucked in measured breaths through his nose. It looked like the thug wasn't getting up in a hurry.

As he started to turn to check on Tracy he caught movement from the corner of his eye and snapped back around, instinctively moving to the side. Hosea had his shirtfront pulled up to expose the handgrip of his revolver, and the fingers of his right hand were on it as he started to pull it clear.

Archer dived forward with the knife outstretched, slamming his bodyweight into Hosea and slapping his gun hand away, ramming the knife into the man's neck with his other hand. The stocky thug jerked beneath him and a jet of blood spurted across the room from his severed carotid artery.

He left the knife in place and rolled aside, grabbing the revolver from Hosea's grasp. Archer fired two rounds at point blank range into Hosea's face, pushed up and turned towards Tracy. Afa was on his side, clearly dead. Tracy kicked him again and his head rolled loosely from a broken neck.

There was no sign of Solomon.

Archer saw the door swinging open and darted to it. The middle-sized thug was limping towards the ute, one hand clapped to his side, the other holding his machete. He heard Archer coming and looked desperately over his shoulder.

'Nooo,' he cried, nearly at the ute now.

Archer raised the Smith and shot him square in the back. Solomon fell forward against the side of the ute and turned, blood frothing at his lips. Archer came closer and shot him again, this time in the chest. Red speckled the white paintwork.

Looking down at the bleeding thug, he could see the terror in his eyes.

'I warned you,' Archer told him coldly. He thumbed the hammer back and squeezed, firing a third shot to the heart.

Solomon was dead before he hit the ground, and Archer returned to the shack.

Tracy was sitting again, still tied to the chair. She was facing the lifeless form of the tall man, Afa. Her face was expressionless and bloodied. Her left eye was almost fully closed and horribly swollen. Her mouth was covered in blood.

Hosea lay still on the floor, the knife in his hand and a fast-expanding pool of blood around him.

'Is he dead?' Tracy whispered thickly.

Archer walked to her side and raised the Smith. He pointed it at Afa's torso and squeezed the trigger. The hammer fell on an empty chamber. Hosea had carried it with only five rounds in the cylinder.

Archer shrugged. 'I don't think it matters,' he said quietly.

He recovered the knife from Hosea's dead fingers and cut Tracy free. She slowly covered herself but otherwise didn't move. Archer searched the two bodies, found nothing of use, then wiped the Smith and Wesson clean and placed it in Hosea's hand, wrapping his fingers round the slick wooden butt.

He wiped the handle of the knife clean too, and placed it near the other outstretched hand. It was a basic attempt to confuse the crime scene, but it should buy them some time.

He quickly gathered the discarded pieces of rope and shoved them in his pocket, along with the long nosed pliers, the extracted tooth and their passports, before helping Tracy up. She moved slowly and painfully as they went outside to the thugs' ute.

Archer helped her into the passenger's seat, took the keys from Solomon's pocket, and checked the vehicle. Their guns and phones were on the floor, and Archer took possession of them. He checked the load in his Beretta and re-holstered it. He also found a water bottle on the floor and offered it to Tracy. She washed her mouth out and spat bloodied water out the window before drinking half of the water and handing the bottle back.

He ripped a piece off his shirt and wet it before gingerly dabbing at the burn on his chest. It stung and throbbed, and he wondered how bad it was. He left the compress on it and held it in place with the seat belt, then drained the bottle and started the ute, manoeuvring round onto the bumpy track and out to the main road.

They needed to get to safety, fast.

40

Half an hour later they entered Apia and dropped the ute in a side street.

The streets were deserted at this hour and the night porter was asleep in the back office, allowing them to slip past quietly and get to their room undisturbed.

Archer locked the door behind them and drew the blinds, turned on plenty of lights and then the TV to cover any noise they made.

Tracy seemed to have withdrawn into herself, so Archer took the lead and organised her. He sat her at the table and fetched the small first aid kit from his suitcase. Kneeling in front of her, he gently took her right hand and placed it on her thigh.

'I'm sorry, this is going to hurt,' he told her, 'but it needs to be done. Bite on this.'

He handed her toothbrush to her and she placed it between her front teeth.

'Breathe in,' he told her, 'be strong and it won't –'

He popped her little finger back into place and her face screwed up in pain as she bit down hard. She was still sucking in her first breath when his fingers moved to the next dislocation and swiftly popped it back into place as well.

A muted scream burst forth from her bloodied lips and tears flowed. Archer shushed her softly and touched her head tenderly, drawing it to his shoulder and letting her cry.

Once she had calmed down, he filled a tea towel with ice cubes from the freezer tray and had her hold it to her left eye. He gave her a glass of water to wash down some strong painkillers, then fetched a flannel from the bathroom and filled a bowl with warm water. He gently dabbed at her face and cleaned her as best he could without causing any more pain. She sat quietly and let him work, whimpering occasionally when he hit a sore spot.

Finally, Archer stood up and brought her a glass of antiseptic mouthwash that he diluted with warm water. He watched as she rinsed her mouth and spat into the sink, cleaning the dried blood from the tooth injury as she did so.

He took her to the bathroom and turned the shower on. Tracy raised her head and looked at him, questions in her eyes.

'Don't be embarrassed,' he said gently, 'you need help and I'm going to help you. It's nothing more than that.' He nodded affirmatively. 'You can trust me, Trace.'

She nodded and cradled her injured hand as he carefully undressed her. Once she was naked he appraised her body, looking for other injuries. She was dirty and blood-stained and covered in bumps and bruises and scratches.

'Here.'

He helped her into the shower and adjusted the heat. He stripped off and put his filthy clothes in a pile with hers, then joined her in the shower. She flinched as he brushed against her and he moved back, giving her space.

He spoke softly and soothingly as he ran his hands through her hair to wet it properly, comforting her through a process he knew she wouldn't be comfortable with but that was necessary nonetheless. He washed her hair first and rinsed it out fully, then took the soap and a flannel and washed her back.

Turning her around, Archer held her by the shoulders and waited for her to look at him. Her eyes were wet and dark, the left one still swollen and painful looking.

'It's okay now,' he told her quietly, 'you're safe with me.'

Tracy nodded slightly and rested her head forward on his chest. She was warm and soft and womanly in his arms.

'I know.' Her voice was barely audible over the running water. 'Thank you.'

Archer finished washing her as quickly and unobtrusively as he could, feeling horribly self-conscious. Once she was clean Archer helped her dress and strapped her fingers, then left her to blow dry her hair while he showered himself.

His own body ached all over and he found new injuries as he washed. He soaped himself thoroughly and scrubbed dried blood off with the flannel, which was now badly stained. The burn was red and yellow and nasty looking, and he made sure he cleaned it out properly, using a small bottle of antiseptic which made his eyes water when it touched the raw wound.

Stepping out and grabbing a towel, he peeked into the bedroom and saw Tracy on the bed, dead to the world, fully dressed. He dressed his wound and rubbed anti-inflammatory cream into his bumps and bruises. He carefully dried himself and dressed in clean cargo pants, a T shirt and boots. He checked his Beretta again and then Tracy's, put the spare ammo in his pocket and then checked the door and windows again.

Satisfied it was all secure, he made himself a strong sweet coffee and took some painkillers before sitting at the table and getting out his cell phone. He badly wanted a real drink, but the coffee would have to do for now. He needed to keep his wits about him.

It was time to make a call.

41

Jonty had sounded croaky when he answered the phone at 3am, but after a minute's talking from Archer he had become wide awake and switched on to what was needed.

Archer gave him precise instructions, told him to hurry, then disconnected and waited. He sat on the sofa with his Beretta ready, Tracy's pistol tucked into his waistband, and the cell phone in his other hand. He had an armchair pulled across the door and felt as ready as he could be. He let sleep take him and awoke with a start to the phone ringing in his hand.

'I'll pick you up in five minutes,' Jonty told him by way of greeting, 'there's a plane waiting.'

He was so keyed in that he seemed like a different man, even dropping his habitual 'y'know.'

Archer woke Tracy, gathered their luggage and led the way out to the front of the hotel. The night porter was still sound asleep in the back of the Reception.

They were just descending the front steps when Jonty pulled up in a red Mercedes SUV. He helped Archer sling the luggage in the back, doing a noticeable double-take when he saw Tracy's injuries, then leaped back in and hit the gas.

As they raced towards the airport, Jonty explained that he had called a local contact and hired him and his plane to make an emergency dash to Auckland. A military medical team would meet them at Whenuapai air base and take them immediately for treatment.

'Re-organise that,' Archer told him, 'I need to get back to London immediately.'

Jonty looked at him in the rear view mirror. After a moment's pause, he nodded his understanding.

'No problem, y'know.'

Jonty did the forty minute trip in twenty five minutes and flew past the terminal to a side gate. As soon as he pulled up the gate swung open and they drove through. The gate clanged shut behind them and a man climbed into the passenger's seat. He was a weathered looking man in his sixties with a white beard.

'Gidday mate,' he greeted Jonty, in a broad Aussie accent. He turned and nodded to the two back seat passengers. 'Alright?'

Archer nodded briefly in response.

'Don't worry mate,' the pilot said cheerfully, 'we've been doin' this for years; you're in safe hands.'

'We?' Archer inquired.

'I've got a doc with me. He'll patch you up a bit before we get there.'

Jonty saw Archer's look and nodded reassuringly. 'It's okay, these guys are solid.'

Ten minutes later they were airborne in a Piper that had seen better days. Jonty had cleansed them – taking all evidence of weapons or equipment used in the assault – and they now just had to wait to land before they could get on with it.

The doctor was an equally old man who Archer picked as the pilot's brother. He was also equally quiet, going about his business efficiently without asking unnecessary questions. He re-dressed Archer's burn before spending more time with Tracy, repeating most of what Archer had already done but doing it better and with superior materials.

The plane was surprisingly well stocked and Archer laid claim to a pre-mixed bottle of bourbon and cola. He would've preferred the alcohol straight but wasn't complaining. The doctor produced some American-issue MREs and prepared one for him. Without being entirely sure what he was eating Archer wolfed it in less than a minute and sat back, nursing his drink and mentally evaluating his injuries.

He wasn't in great shape and he was certain the burn would require some kind of surgery, he was exhausted, and his partner was in worse shape than him. But his mind wouldn't stop buzzing. A million thoughts ran through it, pestering him like mozzies in the jungle.

He felt out of his depth. Self doubt plagued him. This job was like trying to grab smoke *What the fuck am I doing here? This isn't my game. I'm a soldier, not a bloody spook.*

He smiled wryly. What was it that Moore had told him?

It's all smoke and mirrors, mate.

He had that bloody right. He felt like he'd been chasing his tail since the start, always behind the eight ball. Just when he thought he was on top of it the rug got pulled and he was playing catch up again. The enemy were experienced and hard and ruthless, and they always seemed to be half a step ahead.

This was a whole new playing field for Archer, and he felt like he didn't know the rules and was trying to play a traditional game against a team of innovators.

And how the hell did the enemy manage to stay ahead like they did? There was the debacle in Auckland that left a team of cops dead, Boyle's escape after the Cornwall ambush, and now their own capture and torture in Samoa. And who killed Ruth and why? Ability and planning went a long way on the battlefield, cunning and innovation were crucial. But information was the lifeblood of any operation. Intelligence led to planning. Planning led to success. But where did the intel come from? How did the enemy get it?

Was there a leak somewhere? Archer thought back to his discussion with the Director after the Auckland incident, what seemed an age ago. He'd challenged the man directly then, told him there was a leak, but it had really been an accusation based on anger, not fact.

But now he had something to work with. They'd had their legs taken out again and although he had nothing to base his suspicions on, Archer believed he knew where the leak was coming from.

The hard bit was going to be trying to prove it.

Maybe it was time to change, enforce his own rules on the game. Mix it up. *Speed, Aggression, Surprise*; the real SAS.

Archer relaxed back in his seat and let his breath out. He ached all over and was mentally exhausted. He slipped easily into sleep and the next thing he knew they were landing at Whenuapai.

42

An ambulance met them on the tarmac and Tracy was escorted to it, despite her protestations that she was fine. Archer walked her to the back doors and they paused there, neither wanting to take the initiative.

Finally, Archer awkwardly pulled her close and hugged her.

'You're a good girl, Trace,' he whispered in her ear. 'You did well.'

She squeezed him round the neck then kissed him firmly on the cheek and pulled away. Her eyes were wet and tinged with sadness as she looked at him.

'I thought it was all over,' she rasped.

'But it wasn't. You did what you needed to do.' He smiled reassuringly. 'You'll be right as rain before you know it.'

'I gave Matthew up. You need to warn him.'

Archer smiled thinly. 'Don't worry, I'll take care of it.'

She nodded awkwardly, then suddenly grabbed him by the neck and kissed him hard on the lips. Archer blinked with surprise, and then she was gone, turning away and climbing in the back of the ambulance without further ado.

Archer had the distinct feeling he would never see her again. As he watched the ambulance pull away, he felt a twinge of sadness, maybe even regret. He shook his head abruptly and turned his mind back to the job at hand. Subconsciously he was already planning the next move.

He knew exactly where he was going to start.

43

Pimlico was an area favoured by intelligence operatives because of its close proximity to both Vauxhall Bridge and Thames House.

For that very reason Rob Moore had stayed only a month in the flat the firm had organised for him when he moved to London, before getting the hell out and finding a nice one bedroom upstairs flat in Camden. He'd thought himself smart, getting away from the prying eyes and constant paranoia of Pimlico, and it had taken him a further two months to realise the old lady downstairs was the widow of a Special Branch officer.

Not only was she an associate of the intelligence community but he knew for a fact she had allowed operatives from both 5 and Special Branch to search his flat while he was out. They both knew the other knew but he liked the flat, liked Camden and even liked the old bird, so they continued their little dance of pleasantries and innocuous conversation.

At 7pm he unlocked the front door to his flat and pushed the door open with his foot, swinging his daypack in ahead of him in one hand, the other laden with a couple of Tesco's bags.

He was halfway through the door when he realised the alarm

panel in front of him in the vestibule wasn't beeping. He dropped the daypack and started to reach for the door before he felt a presence above him on the stairs.

Archer had a suppressed Sig pointing down at his head. His face was flat and emotionless.

'Come inside, shut the door.'

Moore slowly put the grocery bags down and shut the door behind him. He raised his hands, fighting the urge to look at his daypack. He was unarmed but the bag contained a can of CS spray, and he wondered if he could get his hands on it. It seemed unlikely; Archer had him trapped in the vestibule and would drop him before he'd taken a step.

'Not exactly my normal welcome home,' Moore remarked calmly. His senses were in overdrive but he couldn't tell if Archer was alone.

The barrel of the suppresser didn't move. Archer's gaze remained flat and unforgiving.

'What'd you expect, roses and a nice bottle of red?'

'Well you're acting like a prick and it looks like there'll be claret spilled, so you're not too far wrong,' Moore retorted. 'What the fuck is this about, Arch? You dropped your nuts already?'

'You know what this is about. I've been chasing Will o' the fuckin' Wisp here since the start and I want to know why. I'm tired of the games, Rob. Tell me what the fuck's going on before I jump to the wrong conclusion.'

Moore shook his head. 'I should've known this would bite me in the arse.'

Archer cocked his head inquisitively.

'Not like that, you idiot. *You.* I should've known you were the wrong man for the job. The Director asked my opinion before you were recruited. I recommended you, but it looks like it might the last mistake I make.' He held Archer's gaze. 'For an officer you're not that fuckin' smart, Craig.'

'Really.' The word dripped sarcasm. 'Why don't you educate me then.'

Moore sighed. 'Can I at least put my hands down? I've just done arms and shoulders and I'm seizing up.'

Archer gestured with the gun for him to sit, and Moore slid to the floor against the wall, the door beside him on one side, a shoe rack on the other. A size eleven Cat made a decent weapon, but it wasn't as fast as a 115 grain 9mm Parabellum.

Archer moved half way down the stairs and sat facing him, the Sig held casually. Moore was at a distinct disadvantage here and they both knew it.

'You're sick of chasing ghosts,' Moore said. 'You're grabbing at smoke and always a step behind.' He smiled thinly. 'Welcome to the world of espionage, friend. This is what it's like. Remember what I told you when you first got here?'

'Smoke and mirrors.'

'Exactly. Believe nothing. Trust no one. And always watch your back.'

Archer inclined his head slightly. 'Kinda why I'm here.'

'In the Army it's usually easy to know who you're fighting; they're the ones shooting at you or trying to blow your balls off with an IED. In this world the enemy are usually the least of your worries. It's your friends in the other agencies you've gotta worry about.' Moore shrugged. 'You can't just react to what's happening in front of you, you gotta be thinking five steps ahead. Everyone has their own agenda.'

'So what's yours?'

'The same as it's always been. Protecting New Zealand's interests, working for my government.'

'Who else're you working for?'

'Don't be so naive, mate. I'm one of the good guys, remember? Have you ever questioned my integrity before?'

Archer didn't reply, but he was starting to feel foolish.

'Blades don't go to the bad side mate, so don't even go down that track.' Moore let out his breath and shook his head. 'I'm going to try and open your eyes a bit here, because if you don't sharpen up fast, it'll be game over for you before you even get started.' He gave Archer a hard look. 'And once this is over, you and I are going to clear the air properly. Right?'

Archer gave a brief nod, giving nothing away. 'Crack on.'

Moore cleared his throat and gathered his thoughts before speaking.

'Take this whole thing back to basics; what's it all about?' He ticked points off his fingers. 'It's not idealism. There's no political agenda here. It could be lust, envy, revenge...it could be greed. Thirty two million quid is a lot of dough in anyone's book.'

'It's a drop in the ocean for the Saudis,' Archer pointed out.

'But Yassar's dead, remember? Who benefits from that?'

'He stepped outta line in the family business. He was an embarrassment to them. He had to go.'

'So the Saudis paid Boyle to pop him?'

'Could be.' Even as he said it though, Archer knew he was wrong.

'Possible but unlikely. Boyle's been in it with him, but he's a heavy hitter among these guys. He doesn't need some spineless, snivelling rapist as his running mate. He benefits from Yassar being taken out.'

'Thirty two mill buys a lot of potatoes. But he's not on the inside.'

'Finally.' Moore smiled slightly. 'So look at Boyle. How did he escape? How did he know you were in Samoa?'

The cogs started turning in Archer's head. Moore pressed on.

'Remember he had all night with you guys in Samoa. He could've bled you both dry for hours. Even you would've broken, but Tracy would've given up the Crown Jewels before too much longer.'

'He wanted to know who'd killed the CHIS.'

Moore shook his head. 'No, he wanted you to think that. He asked a question he already knew the answer to.'

Archer stared at him. 'Smoke.'

'Exactly. If this is a game of chess, he doesn't realise he's just a pawn like Yassar. He has a handler.'

'And the handler's on the inside,' Archer realised.

'Mirror mirror, on the wall,' Moore said softly, 'who's the dirtiest of them all?'

44

Many banks around the world were happy to do business with no questions asked, providing financial and other services for the criminals, terrorists and paranoid. One such bank was located in a narrow walkway in the City.

A long-standing customer, Michael Levre, made his way through the security screening at 11am. He was quickly shown to a private windowless room with just a plain table and two chairs for decoration. The bank officer, a slightly built, effeminate Pakistani man, left him with a safety deposit box and closed the door behind him.

Livingstone punched his PIN into the keypad and lifted the lid. Inside was a large plain brown envelope. He ripped it open and dumped the contents on the table.

A Canadian passport and drivers license for Bryan Lawrence, a 45- year old IT consultant from Vancouver. A Visa card in the same name. Two wads of cash-greenbacks and sterling.

He tucked them into the inside pocket of his charcoal suit jacket, re-secured the box and left it where it was. The attendant opened the door as he reached it, which made Livingstone wonder about the presence of hidden cameras. He paused and scanned the room again but still couldn't spot one. Maybe it was just good timing. Maybe he was just paranoid.

Maybe not.

Livingstone nodded to the man and made his way back through the sterile foyer of the bank and out to the grey stone walls of the walkway. A young Polish woman pushing a buggy squeezed past and Livingstone followed her towards the street. The walkway always reminded him of a setting for an old Sherlock Holmes movie, all swirling capes and thick fog and Basil Rathbone looking intense. He let his mind wander for a moment and immediately regretted it.

A heavy wooden door opened on his left as he past it and Archer stepped out. Livingstone caught a fleeting glance of him and had just enough time to open his mouth before a needle slipped effortlessly into his left thigh. His momentum carried him another step forward before his leg buckled and he began to fall.

Archer caught him under the arms and lifted him like a rag doll. Livingstone was aware of it happening but had lost all control of his limbs and his tongue had stopped working. He felt himself dragged backwards through the doorway, the door swung shut and then he was moving down a flight of steps into a dank, cold cellar. Another door shut somewhere above them and heavy feet sounded on the steps. A lone light bulb clicked on above his head. Archer sat him on a chair and moved away into the shadows.

Feeling started to come back to Livingstone's core first and he worked his jaw, rolling his tongue and swallowing. His extremities still felt numb and his thigh ached where that prick had jabbed him.

He waited patiently, knowing that time was both his friend and enemy right now. Rush it and he was done for. Take too long and he was done for. Either way, it was clear he was walking a fine line. Any wrong move would be his last. Livingstone gathered himself mentally, preparing for a final push. This was it. Do or die.

Archer's shadow fell across him as he opened his eyes. The lone bulb cast a weak cone of light in the cold cellar. It had the musty smell of old hops.

'Time to start talking, Livingstone,' Archer said quietly. 'I already know what you've done.'

Livingstone didn't even bother trying to bluster his way out of it. He was a pro and knew when the game was up. Instead, he gave the Kiwi a pompous sneer.

'You may think you know, pal, but you know nothing.' He smirked. 'Besides, there's knowing and there's proving.'

Archer gave a half smile. 'That's true. But we know. We know you had the American contractors on your private payroll; a cell phone number that called them was traced to a shop in Islington. The shop attendant remembered you. Funnily enough, apparently because they wondered why a ponce like you was buying a cheap pre-paid phone. Lesson for the future, I guess.'

Livingstone swallowed but said nothing.

'We know that the 32 mill hidden away by Boyle has disappeared.' He tilted his head and looked at Livingstone. 'Don't s'pose you want to tell me where that went?'

Livingstone felt a lift inside. At least that was a start. He sneered up at the Kiwi. 'If you know so much, why do I need to talk?'

Archer studied him coldly. 'I just don't know why. What was it, Livingstone? Tired of serving your country? Passed over for promotion once too often?'

Livingstone's expression became condescending now, and it occurred to Archer that the man was actually proud of himself.

'Oh no Archer, nothing as fanciful as all that.' He shook his head. 'No no no.'

Archer waited. A soft chuckle escaped Livingstone's throat and he raised his head, looking Archer in the eye and laughing properly now.

'It was much more pure than that, you fool.' Livingstone sighed and his laugh eased. 'Pure, old fashioned greed. Nothing more, nothing less.'

'You caused a lot of aggravation for a lot of people,' Archer said softly. 'Caused a lot of hurt. People got killed because of you.' He gave a small nod. 'By you.'

Livingstone gave a dismissive snort. 'So I have blood on my hands, so what? Who cares? How many men have you killed, Archer? You're like all these gung-ho soldier types, all guns and bombs and killing, kill 'em all and let God sort 'em out!' He sneered again, angry now. 'And you accuse me! You accuse me? What a joke.'

He turned away and snorted, lolling back in the chair, relaxed.

'Do what you're going to do, Archer, whatever it is. But I can guarantee you one thing – I'll not spend a single night in a prison cell.' He sat up now and jabbed a finger at the man before him. 'The British Government cannot allow it to happen. A hero of the security services, a diligent spy who gave his all for his country, fighting terrorism for more than two decades, splashed across the front pages of all the scandal rags. Sent undercover and hung out to dry for the Provos, tortured and suffering Post Traumatic Stress Disorder, an alcohol problem the firm knew about and did nothing to help, death threats from dissident groups that had him living in fear.'

Livingstone's expression was more than confident now. He actually believed what he was saying. He had the arrogance of a man who knew to his very core that he would be facing the firing squad and walking away, maybe not unscathed, but certainly alive.

'You may walk away, but you'll walk away with nothing,' Archer told him.

Livingstone made a scoffing sound. 'So I lose my pension and my shitty flat in Harrow. Woop-de-doo.' He met Archer's flat gaze. 'Take it. It's the least I can do.'

He stood and faced Archer. Arrogance oozed from his pores as he studied the younger man. 'You're a boy in a man's game, son. You'll learn.' He sneered again. 'One day.'

Archer's instinct was to flatten his nose across his pompous, well fed face, but he held himself in check. Instead, he gave a sniff and stepped aside slowly. The invitation was clear. Livingstone made to step past him but was stopped by a hand on his arm.

He stopped, keeping his eyes straight ahead. He felt Archer's breath on his cheek, his voice barely a whisper.

'Count yourself lucky mate. If this was my country, and my rules, there's only one way you'd be leaving this room.'

Livingstone couldn't help himself. 'Yes, well, we're a bit more civilised around here old boy. There's a certain way of doing things.'

He tugged his arm free and walked to the steps, his head high. Archer's voice stopped him again.

'Oh, by the way...that bank in Geneva? They had a slight glitch in their system about five minutes ago.'

Livingstone froze with a foot on the bottom step. He didn't dare turn around.

'Nothing major, just a technical thing, but it appears their firewalls weren't as good as they liked to make out. A certain account is a lot less healthy than it started the day.'

Livingstone could feel Archer's eyes on his back. His heart was racing and he felt faint.

'Not entirely wiped out, but close enough. What's left roughly equates to what your pension fund would be worth.' He gave a small chuckle and Livingstone felt his cheeks flush with humiliation. 'Nothing more, nothing less.'

Livingstone put a shaky foot forward to the next step, unable to breathe properly, and focussed on trying to just keep moving up the steps.

'Best wishes for your retirement.'

45

It had taken three days to get to Thailand, and when he arrived Matthew Livingstone was exhausted.

The stress had taken its toll, the frustration of losing his 32 million – his money – and the discomfort of travelling incognito in cattle class all the way just exacerbated an already deplorable situation.

Still, he reasoned, he was lucky to be alive and lucky to have got away. Good planning over the years had enabled him to have various legends set up that were unknown to his employers. The standard identity set of a passport – preferably Australian, New Zealand or Canadian – a driver's licence and a credit card had been created for him under three different names, and secured in a safe drop box in Essex.

So it was that Andrew Clarke, a 47-year old engineer from the Gold Coast, had arrived in Bangkok with newly-purchased luggage and a wad of cash that got him from the airport to a downtown hotel. He checked in for two nights, immediately ordered a meal and slipped the concierge a crisp $20 greenback to find him a girl for the night.

'Clean,' he told him, 'and young, but not too young.'

Nine hours later, Livingstone was woken by insistent knocking at the door. He fumbled in the dark, feeling for the hooker in the bed but realising she'd gone.

'Bitch,' he muttered, assuming he'd been ripped off. She'd been good but not great, but still.

He turned on the side light and rubbed his eyes, hearing more knocking at the door.

'Hold on,' he called out.

He was trying to pull his trousers on when the door was opened with a key and four men strode in. They were all uniformed members of the police, and two had their guns drawn. Behind them came a fifth man, a white man aged about fifty, dressed in a suit and open-necked shirt.

One of the younger officers moved immediately to Livingstone's luggage on the spare single bed, while two more approached him and snapped instructions in Thai.

He knew better than to resist so put his hands in the air and tried to look non-threatening. His mind raced and he locked eyes with the white man. The white man said nothing, just held him with a cool gaze.

The senior officer stepped up to face him, while his colleagues handcuffed Livingstone's hands behind his back.

'You are under arrest, Mr Lawrence,' he said firmly, and Livingstone felt his heart skip a beat.

At least they don't know who I am.

In the next second, his hopes were crushed.

'Or should I say, Mr Livingstone.' The senior officer was a small man with hard eyes and a flat nose. 'You will come with us.'

'What am I under arrest for?' Livingstone tried to bluster, and the senior officer gave a small, cold smile.

Without even turning his head, he pointed towards his younger colleague who was opening Livinstone's suitcase. 'For that,' he said simply.

Livingstone looked over and saw the younger officer holding up a plastic zip-loc bag of white powder. By the looks of it, it was probably close to a kilo of cocaine or methamphetamine. Livingstone had never seen it before in his life.

He felt his shoulders slump and he looked back towards where the white man had stood a moment ago. He was gone.

The senior officer lost his smile and gave a curt nod.

'Welcome to Bangkok Hilton,' he said.

46

Clifden, County Galway
One month later

Fahey's did a good dinner of a Sunday, and Patrick Boyle had spent many long afternoons there supping pints and enjoying the craic.

He was well known in the area and at Fahey's he was treated as a minor celebrity. The Republican cause was still strong in Connemara and Fahey's had been a focal point of this back in the day.

On this Sunday Boyle had been to Mass in the morning, chatted with Father Gerry for a while afterwards, and slipped the priest a fifty Euro note "for the funds." Father Gerry took it without question and tucked it away beneath his flowing robes.

Boyle walked from the church to Fahey's, taking the time as he did so to make a couple of phone calls. Despite the recent dramas he still had clients waiting for orders and his clients did not like to be kept waiting. He promised them both delivery within a week, agreed to a 10% discount for one due to the delay, and made it to Fahey's bang on midday for lunch.

The barman Sean gave him his first pint on the house, giving a wink as he did so and a 'Good on ya, pal.'

Boyle accepted the drink with a nod and a knowing smile. He raised the glass to his lips and took a long, considered sup. It tasted like nectar, and it was good to be back. He wiped the back of his hand across his mouth and caught the eye of Maura, the waitress.

'The usual, Pat?' she called out in that flirty tone she always used with him, and he nodded and smiled again.

A group of lads were in his usual corner booth, where he could see the doors, and quickly stood when they saw him coming over.

'Alright, lads,' he said, and the lads all nodded and muttered greetings as they shuffled off, vacating the booth for him.

He took his seat and drank while he waited for his dinner. When it came he took his time eating, savouring the tender roast lamb, the perfectly cooked potatoes and the minted peas. The gravy was thick and piping hot and he went heavy on the salt.

Punters came and went, many stopping to say hello or give a wave across the room to him. Boyle replied in kind but today didn't stop to make conversation with anyone. He was in a contemplative mood, and was worried about closing the deals he'd made. Since losing his last shipment, he had nothing on hand right now to fill the orders.

The last month had been spent travelling – London to Bangkok without luck, and home via Malaysia and Singapore. That bastard Livingstone had slipped from his grasp somehow, but Patrick Boyle was determined if nothing else. He would finish the job and avenge both Ruthie's death and the misfortune that had come to him.

Another Guinness chased the meal down and eventually Boyle sat back and wiped his mouth on his napkin, full and satisfied.

He left cash on the table to cover the bill, gave a wave to Maura and a nod to Sean, and walked out of the pub, heading for home.

Five minutes later he wheeled the blue Pajero into the yard of his farmhouse and parked beside the shed. The chooks were running loose and sheep grazed in the paddocks beyond the white-washed house. The farm had been in the family for generations now and still had the original stone walls. It was peaceful out here and his closest neighbours were four hundred yards away. They were reclusive artists – she painted, he wrote poetry – and they gave him no bother.

Boyle crossed to the front door, whistling for the dog. He was probably off chasing rabbits, Boyle thought, reaching for the door handle.

His right arm suddenly jerked and he felt a thump and heard a tiny *phhtt* at the same time. He grabbed at his forearm, feeling blood already coming through the sleeve of his jacket, and knew he'd been shot.

He spun on his heel to go for the Pajero, letting go of the wounded arm and scrabbling under his jacket with his left hand. His Browning was holstered under his left arm and it was awkward to get to with that hand.

As he moved, he knew it was already too late, but Patrick Boyle never went down without a fight.

His fingers closed around the butt of the Browning, and he saw the Kiwi step from behind the shed twenty metres away. He was clad in DPMs with a floppy bush hat, and had an M4 slung across his back. A suppressed Sig was in his grip, pointing towards Boyle.

Despite the situation they were in, Boyle couldn't help but appreciate it had been a hell of a shot with a suppressor from that distance.

'Leave it,' Archer ordered him, advancing across the yard.

Boyle glowered at him and continued trying to tug the pistol free.

Archer squeezed the trigger again and put a round through Boyle's left shoulder, blasting straight through the joint and ripping it apart. The impact spun him half around and caused him to stagger. His left hand dropped uselessly to his side and he cursed.

Archer moved closer, barely four metres away now, the Sig still raised. 'You had your chance,' he said quietly.

Boyle scowled at him. 'Go to hell,' he growled. 'Are ye here to talk?'

Archer considered him for a moment.

'No,' he said softly, and fired a double tap into Boyle's mouth.

The body crumpled and fell in a heap on the ground. Blood

began to leak from beneath the head and lifeless eyes stared into the distance.

Archer stepped forward over the body, and looked down at it.

He felt neither regret nor guilt. It was just a lump of meat and fabric now. A bird twittered somewhere in the sky above him.

He raised the Sig and put a third round into the side of the head. The body twitched with the impact then lay still.

Archer bent and picked up his spent brass, pocketed it, and walked away.

Job done.

END

For more information or other thrilling adventures, jump over to
www.writerangusmclean.com
or grab the latest from Amazon.

And if you enjoyed *Smoke and Mirrors*,
please leave a review to let me know.

BONUS CHAPTERS
THE DIVISION #2

Call to Arms

47

Jack Travis saw the visitor well before he got to his front door and pushed himself up from the dining table, putting down his pen and picking up his coffee mug.

The blue Hyundai Sonata bumped down the gravel farm driveway from the road, approaching the weatherboard bungalow slowly and pulling up near the open detached garage. A forest green Holden Colorado double cab ute was parked inside, splashed with mud.

A Honda quad bike stood nearby. A border collie barked and ran from the porch, wagging his tail excitedly and watching as the visitor alighted from the vehicle.

He was a medium sized man with sandy hair and an unremarkable face, dressed casually in chinos and a black Kathmandu jacket. When he walked he had a slight but noticeable limp, and he carried himself stiffly.

Jed Ingoe – known as Jedi – had been the Regimental Sergeant Major of 1NZSAS Group until he lost part of his leg in an IED incident in Afghanistan. Invalided from the Army, he had traded being one of the hardest men to ever wear the sand beret to being the Operations Officer for Division 5 of the Security Intelligence Service.

Known as The Division, it was the most covert unit of the security service. The former Special Forces operators it employed carried out the dirty work of the Government, the blackest of the black operations. The stuff that needed to be done to keep the playing fields level – within reason – between the good guys and those that sought to disrupt peace.

Ingoe never did anything without reason, and so it was today that he came cold calling on Jack Travis. He turned his gaze from the rolling farmland to the paddocks closer to the house. A couple contained heifer calves and chooks pecked around another near a coop. He saw that the ground dropped away from the other side of the house to a pond where a few ducks swam lazily. A small creek ran through the property and fed the pond.

Beside the house was a large vegetable garden behind a trellis fence, a smaller herb garden adjacent to it. Citrus and other fruit trees grew on the other side of the house and a grape vine had spread itself along a fence. The house was on tank water and he could see a couple of solar panels on the roof.

Ingoe turned back to the house itself, which was in need of a fresh coat of paint. A pair of muddy gumboots stood by the door, which was open. An oilskin coat hung on a hook above the boots.

A man stood in the doorway. He was six foot and strongly built, a few years younger than Ingoe. Receding dark hair going to grey and clipped very short, unshaven and with an outdoorsman's complexion. He wore faded jeans and his checked flannel shirt was hanging out. A steaming cup of coffee was in one hand, the other tucked in his pocket. He was watching Ingoe.

Ingoe's stoic expression creased into a smile and he moved forward, hand extended.

'Good to see you, Jack.'

'You too.' Travis gave his hand a short, hard pump. He smiled and moved inside. 'Come in, I've just made a pot.'

Ingoe followed him in through an open living area into a large farm-style kitchen. Classic rock was coming from a stereo in the lounge. Ingoe wasn't too up with the play with the genre – if it wasn't about cowboys and lost love and life on the range, he didn't want to know. Travis took another mug from a cupboard and filled it from the machine on the bench. He gave it to Ingoe and gestured for him to take a seat at the breakfast bar.

Ingoe did so and took a sip. It was black and strong. French doors opened from the dining area onto a wide deck that overlooked the rolling green farmland. Ingoe admired the view for a moment. 'Machine coffee,' he commented. 'You going all Ponsonby on us, Jack?'

Travis smiled again. 'Just like good coffee.' He flicked a nod towards his visitor's leg. 'How's the leg?'

Ingoe shrugged. 'It is what it is. I get by.' He took another sip and put his mug down. 'Living off the grid yet?'

'Working on it.' Travis used a remote to turn down the stereo. 'It's everybody's dream isn't it?'

Ingoe changed tack. 'Been back long?' Travis gave him a sharp look and Ingoe grinned.

'A month. I had six months in Iraq and two in Syria.'

'Residential?' He was referring to residential security, a common role in trouble spots for former operators on the Circuit.

'Some, plus escorting some news crews.' Travis gave a small grin. 'Interesting times.'

Ingoe nodded, warming his hands on the mug. 'Seen the news?'

'Yep.' Travis gestured towards the morning's paper spread out on the dining table. A laptop stood open beside it, with a notepad and pen. The pad had brief notes jotted down.

Ingoe nodded. 'Big news.'

'Bad news. Sounds organised.'

'Very.'

'How many dead?'

Ingoe paused, considering his response. 'More than what the media say.'

'They've said a security guard, three cops and two civilians dead, plus one baddie. And five cops and four more civvies wounded.' Travis watched him, assessing his reply.

'That's true. Probably two more casualties for the bad guys though, we think one dead if not both.'

Travis let out a low whistle. 'That's some serious fire fight. And in downtown Wellington too.'

'And about twenty million bucks worth of gold bullion taken.'

Travis whistled again. 'They had a machine gun and grenades and an RPG?'

'Yep.'

Travis sipped his own coffee before crossing to the pantry and taking out a biscuit barrel. Ingoe took one and examined it with a wry grin.

'Anzac biscuits?'

'Made with my own hand.' Travis took a bite of one and they both chewed in silence for a minute. 'So this isn't a social call then.'

Ingoe put his biscuit on the benchtop. 'No,' he said carefully. 'All that ordnance came from somewhere, and the bullion is going somewhere too.'

'Sounds like a job for the cops, not our...your outfit.'

Ingoe tilted his head slightly. 'In theory. There's an international angle to it though.'

'And? You don't need me. The Boss made it pretty clear I wouldn't be coming back.'

Ingoe met his gaze. 'The cops involved. They were STG.'

Travis paused. Ingoe continued.

'One of them took out three of the bad guys.' Ingoe met his gaze calmly. 'Your nephew.'

Travis felt a kick in his chest and put his mug down. 'Brad.'

Ingoe's Hyundai was disappearing out onto the winding road to make his way from Onewhero back across the river towards Tuakau. Travis stood on the deck and watched it go, emptying his mug, his brow furrowed.

He turned back inside and glanced at the notes he'd been making when his former boss had arrived. The robbery and subsequent shootout was headline news worldwide and he had followed it closely over the last several hours. Experience had told him it was more than a bunch of hoods robbing a cash-in-transit van, as had been told to the media.

Experience. From joining the Army as a boy to eighteen years in the Group, ending up as a Squadron Sergeant Major – Warrant Officer Class 2, and next in line for the RSM position after Ingoe's tragedy. Next in line, that was, until his run in with an obnoxious Air Force pilot. The pilot had objected to being taken to task over his recklessness and Travis had objected to a twenty six year old officer trying to put him in his place.

The result was a broken nose for the pilot and a pending court martial for Travis. It could have been dealt with had the pilot not been the son of a senior Cabinet Minister. His exit without charges had been arranged quickly and Travis found himself out in the cold, thrown into work on the Circuit with former comrades from all arms of the forces round the world.

The last year had been a journey of intense self-discovery for the tough former SSM, and he had planned on taking some time out to get his property operating how he wanted it to be. His remark to Ingoe about living off the grid wasn't too far from the truth; the attraction was strong, although he was realistic enough to know that to be completely self-sufficient was a big ask and very time consuming.

He had heifers and chickens, sufficient fruit and vegetables all year round, and a good trade arrangement with neighbours who ran sheep and pigs. Seasonal hunting helped keep the freezers full.

But as he watched the Hyundai disappear from sight down the winding country road, Travis knew without a doubt that he was about to step back into the fold.

He'd let his nephew down before; he wouldn't do it again.

Lightning Source UK Ltd.
Milton Keynes UK
UKHW020645280322
400716UK00007B/187

9 780473 560843